GAWEN'S CLAIM

HIGHLANDER FATE, LAIRDS OF THE ISLES BOOK ONE

STELLA KNIGHT

Copyright © 2019 by Stella Knight

All rights reserved.

This book or any portion thereof may not be reproduced, or stored in a retrieval system, or transmitted in any form or by any means, electronic, mechanical, photocopying, recording, or otherwise, without the express written permission of the publisher.

stellaknightbooks.com

This is a work of fiction. Names, characters, organizations, places, events, and incidents are either products of the author's imagination or used fictitiously.

Cover Design by Kim Killion

PRONUNCIATION GUIDE

Gawen - GOW-in
Siobhan - shi-VAWN
Aonghus - AIN-gus
Achdara - ASH-dawr-uh
Mysie - MIE-see
Inghean - IHN-jiy-in
Coira - KAWR-uh
Kudan - KU-dun
Ysenda - IH-send-ah
Malmuira - MAEL-my-ruh
Sgaire - SKAW-ruh

CHAPTER 1

Present Day
Isle of Skye, Scotland

"I've detected an anomaly in the strands of time."

Lila went absolutely still at the words, her heart pounding against her ribcage. The woman who'd spoken, Siobhan, stood at the head of the drawing room, holding the gazes of each man and woman who sat before her.

Lila clenched her trembling hands in her lap, sucking in a breath. The men and women gathered in Siobhan's drawing room were all *stiuireadh*—descendants of druid witches who had the ability to travel through time. When you had the ability to travel through time, there wasn't much that could shock you. But Siobhan's words caused shock to ripple through the room.

"I've used Locator spells to try and determine the exact time and place of this anomaly," Siobhan continued, her brow furrowing with worry.

Siobhan was in her late forties, a willowy woman with dark hair and intelligent hazel eyes. As head of their coven, Siobhan was always the face of calm; Lila had never seen her look even mildly concerned before.

"The closest I could get was to May 1395, here on the Isle of Skye. I believe it's another witch causing this anomaly. Only someone with our powers can do such a thing."

Siobhan paused, allowing a moment for her words to sink in before she continued.

"This anomaly is the reason I've called this coven meeting. I need one of you to travel back to this time and stop this dark witch, whoever he or she is. There were several clans on the island at this time; all have partaken in the Pact. My Locator spells have placed this dark witch on the north part of the island—the seat of the MacRaild clan. Gawen MacRaild, laird and chief, has already been contacted and is prepared to assist whoever we send."

Gawen MacRaild. For some reason, a sense of familiarity settled over Lila at the mention of the name, though she was certain she'd never heard it before. Whoever this Gawen was, he knew of magic, time travel, and witches . . . all because of the Pact.

Centuries ago, a coven of stiuireadh had helped the chieftains of the Western Scottish Isles ward off waves of invaders from the north, who'd ignored a peace treaty signed between the kings of Scotland and Norway and continued to pillage. As an act of gratitude for their assistance, the chieftains had vowed to assist the stiuireadh in return. Every descendant of these chieftains of the isles—and those stiuireadh—had the ancient Pact drilled into their memory.

We, the lairds and chieftains of the isles, vow to forever assist the stiuireadh in their quest to protect the strands of time and humanity from those who seek destruction.

Lila swallowed hard, her pulse thrumming against the base of her throat. She needed to volunteer. This was the opportunity she'd been seeking for years. She'd traveled to the year 1395 before with her sister, Avery, and she was familiar with the Isle of Skye, having visited with her family many times over the years.

"Is there anyone who is willing to—"

Lila was on her feet before Siobhan could finish her sentence. She could feel her blood rushing through her veins as every eye in the room landed on her. But she held her head high, even at the looks of disbelief—and amusement—on the faces of the other witches. She knew what they were all thinking. Lila Fletcher, the weak daughter of those powerful American witches, Isaac and Karen? Why not her stronger sister, Avery? Why not her parents?

"I'll do it," Lila said firmly, continuing to ignore their stares.

To her relief, Siobhan wasn't looking at her with disbelief or amusement. She didn't look surprised at all, as if she'd expected her to volunteer.

"My parents are vacationing in Bermuda, and my sister is on one of her time-traveling field trips; I believe she's in the seventeenth century. Or the nineteenth. That's—that's why they couldn't attend this meeting," Lila continued, hating the way her voice wavered with defensiveness.

"I'm aware of the whereabouts of your family," Siobhan said, giving her a patient smile, and Lila flushed with embarrassment. Of course, Siobhan knew where her family was; she was a Time Seer—a *fiosaiche*. Only Seers could serve as heads of covens; they were the only ones who could detect anomalies in the fabric of time and were the best at Locator spells. But this also meant that they could rarely travel through time; their magic worked best when they remained in the time in which they were born.

"Why do you want to go back?" Siobhan asked now, her dark eyes probing Lila's.

Because I need to prove to all of you, myself, and my family that I deserve to be a stiuireadh. That I'm just as strong as my family, or any of you, Lila thought, with a flash of defiance.

"I've been to that year before with my sister," Lila said instead. "Avery wanted to explore what a young Edinburgh was like in that time. And I'm familiar with Skye; I've been here many times."

"Being familiar with the year, and the island,

isn't good enough," Fergus Cattenach, one of the older members of the coven, snapped. "We need someone powerful enough to locate and take on this dark witch who's wreaking havoc with time. We know that your parents and sister are strong with Time magic, but none of us have seen you demonstrate such power."

Several others murmured words of agreement, and a surge of uncertainty flooded Lila's body. To her surprise, it was Siobhan who spoke up to defend her.

"This undertaking is not about a show of power," Siobhan said. "Once Lila locates this dark witch, if she's unable to defeat her using her magic, she can send for another witch from the coven to assist her. But for now, we can only send one. This witch may be able to sense if another stiuireadh is trying to stop her; we need to keep our presence in this time to a minimum."

Disappointment coursed through her; *she* wanted to be the one to destroy the dark witch. But she made herself remain silent. She needed them to agree to send her back, so she wouldn't offer any protests.

"Does that sound agreeable, Lila?" Siobhan asked.

"Yes."

"Are there any other objections to sending Lila back?" Siobhan asked. Her tone was light, but there was no mistaking the challenge in her words.

Lila braced herself for the barrage of protests. But no one, not even the sour-faced Fergus, interjected. None of them wanted to argue with Siobhan, the most powerful among them—and their leader. The tension ebbed from Lila's shoulders as Siobhan turned back to face her.

"Well, Lila," Siobhan said, giving her a wide smile, "let's get you prepared for the fourteenth century."

LILA FLED to her guest room after the meeting, wanting to escape the dismissive looks of the other witches. She didn't know if the reason for their hostility was because they themselves had wanted to go, or if they didn't trust her to carry out the tasks. *Or both,* Lila grimly thought to herself.

Lila had grown up learning all about the magic in her bloodline, of their incredible ability to travel through time. She'd eagerly waited until she came of age, the only time her protective parents would let her and Avery travel, to take her first trip through time.

She and Avery had traveled to the year 1922; it was the earliest time period their parents initially allowed them to travel to. She'd taken in every detail of the past with awe. Avery had shared her delight, but her parents had always warned them of the limits—and dangers—of time travel.

Yet what she'd learned most of all was her lack of power compared to her parents or her sister. The spells, which came easily to them, were a struggle for Lila. And if she wasn't with Avery, it was difficult for her to issue the complex spells required to travel through time. In fact, she'd never traveled through time on her own: Avery had always accompanied her.

Shame roiled through her at the thought. Avery and her parents had continually insisted that she was just as strong as they were; it was her own self-doubt limiting her abilities, but Lila thought they were just being kind. She wanted—needed—to prove to herself that she was strong.

Lila expelled a sigh, glancing over at her cell phone resting on the side table next to the bed. Her parents would be worried sick once they knew where and when she was going. And she had no idea how long she'd be in the past. Weeks? Months? *Years?* She knew there were witches who stayed in the past for long periods of time; she'd even heard of witches who'd fallen in love with men and women in the past and chosen to stay.

Lila had no intention of staying. As much as she enjoyed her jaunts to the past, she was too fond of the conveniences of modern-day life. She just wanted to carry out her task, prove her worth, and return all the stronger for it.

Lila gritted her teeth, deciding to get the dreaded phone call to her parents over with. She wished Avery was with them; her sister was always good at reeling in their protective instincts. But Avery was off on one of her time-traveling jaunts. Avery loved traveling through time, even more so than Lila. She couldn't help but smile at the thought of her adventurous sister. As envious as she'd been of Avery over the years, she loved her dearly, and missed her whenever she traveled on her own.

She picked up the phone and dialed her father's number, praying they were snorkeling or exploring the island and she could just leave a voice mail. But her father answered on the first ring.

"It's good to hear your voice, sweetheart," her father's voice boomed over the line. "How was the meeting?"

"It was . . . eventful," she replied, and told him about the anomaly Siobhan had detected.

"Ah," her father said, after a brief pause. "Who's going back to deal with it? It's too bad your sister is off on one of her adventures—she would've loved to do something like this."

That old, familiar jealousy swelled in her chest. She tamped it down, reminding herself that her father meant no harm . . . and he was right. This task would be a cinch for Avery.

She took a deep breath; it was time to change their perception of her. To change her perception of herself.

"I am."

The pause on the other end of the line went on for so long that she feared she'd dropped the call. When her father spoke again, his voice was hard: a tone that had frightened her when she was a little girl.

"You most certainly are not," he snapped. "You will get on a plane this instant and—"

Before Lila could reply, angry self-defense rising in her gut—she was twenty-six years old, for God's sake, and her father had scolded her like she was a misbehaving child—her mother's calm voice came on over the line.

"What your father is trying to say," her mother said, "is that he loves you very much, and he's worried. The only reason your father suggested Avery is because she's done something like this before, so—"

"And I can as well," Lila snapped, her patience wearing thin. "How do you think I've always felt, knowing that I'm not as powerful as the rest of you? Never feeling like I belonged?"

Despite herself, her voice caught, and she closed her eyes against the hot sting of tears.

"Oh, sweetheart," her mother breathed, concern shaping her voice. "We've always told you—"

"I know what you've always told me," Lila interjected, her voice rising with determination, "and since I'm an *adult* who makes her own decisions, I'm going back in time to find this dark witch. And I'm going to stop her."

CHAPTER 2

1395
Carraig Castle
Isle of Skye, Scotland

"When will the stiuireadh arrive?" Aonghus asked.

Gawen didn't look up from the flames of the fireplace, taking a sip of his ale.

"On the morrow," he grumbled, irritation coursing through him at the thought of this witch who would soon disrupt the steady pace of his daily routine.

"I can tell by the look of ye how happy this makes ye," Aonghus said, his dark eyes twinkling with amusement.

Gawen shot his steward a look of annoyance, taking another swig of ale; ale which wasn't strong enough. He and Aonghus were gathered in his private study where they could talk of such matters—magical matters—without being overheard.

He'd been in a foul mood ever since a letter had appeared in his study, written in halting Gaelic by Siobhan, a stiuireadh from a time in the future, informing him of a dark witch's presence on his lands, and the pending arrival of a stiuireadh to stop her. She'd reminded him of the old Pact his ancestors had made.

He'd scowled at the letter, both unnerved and irritated at this stiuireadh's ability to communicate with him through time. There was a time when he would have been happy, perhaps even eager, to assist these mystical, time-traveling witches. But now he felt only bitterness and resentment at the thought. It was only his concern over her mention of a dark witch—an *aingidh*—on his lands that made him heed the letter.

Recently, two farmers had been found murdered on his lands. The men he'd had investigate informed him their murders were likely the result of a dispute over cattle or land. Gawen had suspected there was more to these murders. There were disputes all the time on his lands, but they rarely resulted in murder. A chill crept along his skin. What if the murders were because of this dark witch Siobhan mentioned?

"I'll do my duty when she arrives," he muttered. "If I need tae leave the castle tae assist her, will ye—"

"I'll handle things here. Ye need nae worry,"

Aonghus assured him, and Gawen's sour mood ebbed—somewhat.

As his steward, Aonghus ran the castle with smooth efficiency. He'd been vital during the past three years as Gawen's grief had immersed him in self-imposed solitude, and it had proved increasingly difficult to tend to castle matters.

But he knew the time for his self-imposed solitude had come to an end. Before the stiuireadh's visit, he'd begun preliminary discussions with his nobles about taking a bride. He would need an heir, and at thirty-two he was getting older. As the last surviving member of his family, it was imperative that he continue the bloodline.

The thought of marriage brought him no joy. He would make it clear to his bride that their marriage was only a matter of duty. Once she bore him sons, she would have her own life as he would have his. After suffering the loss of his beloved parents and sister, Gordana, during a small outbreak of plague three years ago, he was leery of forming emotional ties to anyone. The very thought of losing a future bairn sent a wave of fear roiling through his belly.

His grip tightened on his cup of ale. After his family's deaths, he'd sent for a stiuireadh, knowing they could manipulate time. He'd begged her to change the past to save his family's lives. She'd insisted that this was something that time wouldn't allow to change.

Some things that have already happened simply must be, she'd said, giving him a sorrowful look.

Fury swept over him at the memory. He'd heard

tales of some people—and stiuireadh—changing the events of the past. As far as he knew, the stiuireadh made their own rules about what could and could not be changed. It was something he'd never forgive them for, these witches who manipulated time. It wasn't natural. After receiving Siobhan's letter, he'd considered informing her that he had no intention of helping one of her kind.

But he couldn't let himself break the Pact, that ancient promise that his ancestors had held so dear. And the Pact had meant a great deal to his father, who'd held the stiuireadh and their abilities in great reverence. Would he still hold such reverence for them if he knew they wouldn't prevent his death, or the deaths of his wife and daughter?

"Traveling through time," Aonghus mused, pulling Gawen from the maelstrom of his thoughts. "I cannae fathom it. To see a different year? A different century?"

Gawen scowled at the reverence in Aonghus's tone. Like other high-ranking members of his clan, Aonghus had learned of the stiuireadh when he was a lad. There weren't many who knew of the ancient Pact and the existence of these witches; it was a carefully guarded secret, only passed down to certain sons by their fathers, brother to brother, cousin to cousin. The knowledge of witches who could manipulate time was a dangerous thing; there were many who believed that all witches were evil and must be destroyed.

"'Tis unnatural," Gawen said, taking another swig of his ale. "It doesnae matter, Aonghus. They donnae need our worship. I will do my duty tae assist this stiuireadh and then send her back tae the time in which she belongs."

"Do ye think she'll be bonnie?" Aonghus asked, unperturbed by Gawen's hard tone. He gave Gawen a teasing look. "A bonnie lass will—"

"No," Gawen said shortly. He'd seen only three stiuireadh in his lifetime; each one had been decades older than him and reminded him of his departed Nan, with her stooped shoulders and ash-gray hair. "And it doesnae matter if she is bonnie—the stiuireadh arenae tae bed. When they come tae a different time, 'tis only tae carry out a duty."

He stood, setting down his ale on the mantle of the fireplace. His study had suddenly become stifling, and he was weary of discussing the stiuireadh. He needed air.

"I'm going for a ride."

He felt Aonghus's eyes on him as he left the study. Aonghus knew him better than anyone; they'd been friends since they were lads, since before Aonghus had stepped into his own father's position as steward of Carraig Castle. Aonghus was one of the few men who'd seen Gawen weep over the loss of his parents and dear sister. He'd clamped his hand on Gawen's shoulder and gruffly told him to allow himself to grieve; Gawen had feared he'd shame him for his weakness. He was grateful every day for Aonghus's presence. After his family's death, Aonghus was the only person he was close to.

He was on his way out of the castle when a tall, blonde woman, Achdara, intercepted him. There was a time when he would have been happy to see her, but now he stiffened. They had exchanged a few drunken kisses after feasts in the past, and he'd considered courting her before the deaths of his family. She'd pretended to sympathize after their deaths, but he'd realized her concern was a façade—she'd only wanted the status of becoming lady of his castle, wife of the laird and chieftain. She had since wed, and subsequently been widowed, by a wealthy merchant. Yet she made her continued sexual interest in him clear, though he no longer had any interest in her.

"Laird MacRaild," she said, stepping so close he could smell the cloyingly sweet rosewater scent of her hair, a scent he usually found enticing

"Lady McNabb," he coolly returned, emphasizing her late husband's name.

She tensed at the formal use of her name, before the sultry smile returned to her lips. She took another step closer to him; he resisted the urge to step back.

"Are ye off for a ride, my laird? Perhaps I can join ye?"

"I thank ye, but I'd prefer tae take my ride alone," he said, forcing a polite smile. "Good day tae ye. I'll see ye at the feast."

He swept past her before she could offer a protest, glad to be out of her stifling presence. He was relieved that he'd not gone through with courting her; there was a coldness to her he'd not noticed before.

Moments later, he rode away from the castle,

relishing in the damp air on his skin as he made his way to the old cemetery south of the castle grounds. A fresh rain had fallen, and the sky was a somber gray, though hints of sunlight broke through the clouds, illuminating the green countryside that surrounded him.

He soon arrived at the cemetery, and after tying up his horse to a nearby tree, he walked to the familiar stone markers of his family's resting place. He knelt before their graves, placing a hand on the damp earth and closing his eyes.

He'd been uncommonly close with all three of them; he hunted every week with his father, took walks with his mother and sister, and always sat at their sides during feasts in the great hall. His parents had been getting on in years and preparing to step down from their roles as laird and lady, expressing their desire to return to his mother's ancestral manor in the Highlands to live out their remaining years, leaving the castle to Gawen and whoever he chose for his wife. Gordana had been looking forward to getting wed and starting a family of her own, playfully ignoring her older brother's protectiveness when it came to her suitors.

I cannae wait for ye tae meet the lass ye'll wed, she'd chided him. *Ye'll be tae focused on her tae worry about yer wee sister.*

He could remember every detail of the last feast they'd enjoyed together. It had been during Yule; he and Gordana had watched their parents dance in the center of the great hall before getting up to dance themselves. There had been such joy on their faces, such ignorance of the tragedy soon to come.

The outbreak of plague had swept over the castle like a storm, first affecting the peasants who lived just outside the castle, then the servants, then the nobles. Local healers didn't know the cause, or how to stop it. Many, like Gawen himself and Aonghus, weren't affected by the illness, but when it passed, two dozen nobles and servants had died, including his parents and Gordana.

He'd stayed at their bedsides even after they'd passed, grief wracking his body as he took in their still forms, wondering how they could suddenly be gone. That was when he'd sent for the stiuireadh, begging her to change what had happened. *This is something that can't be changed*, she'd insisted, before leaving him alone in his study, shaken and utterly broken.

He closed his eyes, willing away his anger at the stiuireadh, before getting to his feet.

I'll do this for ye and only for ye, Father, he silently vowed, looking down at his father's marker. *And then my duty to the stiuireadh is done. I'll nae help them again.*

CHAPTER 3

Present Day
Isle of Skye, Scotland

"The threads of time aren't always fixed," Siobhan said, flipping through the pages of her grimoire. "Sometimes they can shift and weave. I know of many travelers who've gone back to reverse tragedies that have occurred: those are the lucky ones. But there are other events that must happen—those are the things that shouldn't be changed."

Lila and Siobhan were seated across from each other in Siobhan's study, which was tiny and overstuffed with grimoires and other ancient-looking books. They'd been here for most of the morning, with Siobhan reviewing the spells Lila would need to perform in the past.

Lila considered Siobhan's words as she took a sip of her hot tea. She'd heard this before. When one had the ability to travel through time, it was tempting to go back and change major world events for the better. There had been witches and travelers who'd tried, all with dire consequences. Some things were simply meant to happen—from events as seemingly minor as a car accident to major events such as wars or revolutions. One of the first lectures her parents had given her and Avery had been warning them of the dangers of attempting to change things in the past that time—or fate—needed to happen. One ancestor of theirs had foolishly attempted to prevent the First World War and had simple ceased to exist. Another had attempted to prevent the death of her husband and ended up dying herself.

You must never attempt to change what must happen, her mother had warned her and Avery. *Only those events which are malleable in the fabric of time can be changed. That is why stiuireadh take the council of the fiosaiche; they can see what can and cannot be changed.*

"If this dark witch is attempting to change something that can't be changed—why are we trying to stop her ourselves? Won't Time itself turn on her, the way it has with others?" Lila asked now, her brow furrowed.

"Sometimes—rarely—if a witch is powerful enough, and with the right spells, some events not meant to change can indeed change. But always with dire consequences to other events, people, and to the witch themselves. She's already changed something; it's why I was alerted to her presence. Whatever this dark witch—this aingidh—did, it was evil. She murdered or otherwise harmed someone who shouldn't have been. We need to stop her before she can do any more harm."

A shiver snaked along Lila's spine at the word "aingidh," derived from the Gaelic word for wicked, the coven's term for a witch who used her magic for dark purposes.

Lila wasn't naïve; she knew there were witches who used their ability to perform dark magic. She'd heard many tales of such witches. Power like theirs was easily corruptible.

"This grimoire," Siobhan said, sliding it across the table toward Lila, "contains very old spells, ones which should work better for you in the past. I know you're somewhat familiar with Skye, but I have some old maps of the island that the coven's historian prepared; I'd like for you to review it. And Lila," Siobhan hedged, a look of concern flickering across her features, "I know this is a lot to take in, given that we need you to leave in two days. If it's too much—"

"No," Lila said quickly—too quickly—forcing a smile. "I'll be ready."

She had to be.

Siobhan studied her for a long moment, as if not quite believing her, before reaching out to take both her hands.

"I know it's difficult, coming from a family of powerful witches. I'm not the strongest in my own family."

Lila looked at her in disbelief. The fiosaiche were especially powerful witches. She found it hard to believe that Siobhan didn't possess great power.

As if reading her thoughts, Siobhan smiled.

"Power is relative, especially among our kind," she said. "Just remember that every witch has their own distinctive power. And I think you—" Siobhan began, but stopped abruptly. Her brow furrowed, and she looked as if she wanted to say something more. "You'll do well," she said finally, leaving Lila to ponder what she'd stopped herself from saying. "Let's take a break; the coven historian wants to go over some things with you. Then we can practice more Locator spells."

For the rest of the day, Lila worked with both Siobhan and the coven historian, Madeline, who reviewed the basics of the time period with her.

"I've already been to 1395," Lila grumbled to Madeline, eager to get back to practicing spells. "Is all this reviewing necessary?"

"Staying in ruddy inns with your sister is different from staying in a castle where everyone will notice you. You need to remember—just because Laird MacRaild knows what you are, not everyone does. You need to fit in as seamlessly as possible."

Lila dutifully fell silent as Madeline went over court dances of the time and made her repeat her backstory until she knew it backward and forward: she was an old friend of Laird MacRaild's family, visiting from England and staying at the castle for a time as his honored guest.

When she wasn't with Madeline, she was with Siobhan as she practiced Locator spells. Her magic was passable; she was able to locate the objects Siobhan directed her to using spells, but finding an object was far different from finding a person. Still, she made herself show confidence she didn't feel, issuing spell after spell, from Levitation spells—lifting a grimoire from Siobhan's desk—to more complex ones such as Concealing spells—concealing the same grimoire from view.

After they'd finished for the day and had a quick dinner, Siobhan seemed satisfied and urged her to get some rest.

Lila returned to her guest room, bone tired. She hadn't wanted to show Siobhan what a toll performing spells had taken on her; the more powerful the witch, the less of a toll his or her magic took. Her eyes were heavy, and she fell into a deep sleep as soon as her head hit the pillow.

Her dreams were a torrent of vivid activity. She saw the vague features of a handsome man whose visage filled her with warmth—and a longing that was almost painful.

She stood on the edge of a cliff, terror racing through her as she looked down at the sheer drop to the ocean below.

She saw the briefest flash of a woman's face, too distant and vague for her to clearly make out her features, but in that brief moment a powerful sense of grief and fury seized her.

When she awoke, a sob of grief tore from her,

and she didn't know where the grief had come from.

Lila looked around her bedroom, wide eyed and trembling. Could the image of that woman be the dark witch they were looking for? If so, why did she appear in her dream? Why had she felt that grief and rage?

Her hands were still shaky as she made herself shower, trying to luxuriate in the droplets of warm water on her skin—this may be the last shower she'd enjoy for some time. But her unease had settled in on her like a great weight; she could barely concentrate as she changed into the underdress and blue gown Madeline had provided for her, before styling her hair into the late-fourteenth-century style of two braided buns wound through with ribbons.

When she went down to the entryway to meet Siobhan, she tried to keep her features neutral. She was relieved that the other witches had already left, that she only had Siobhan to contend with. But she was a terrible actress because Siobhan's features instantly creased with concern.

"Is everything all right?" Siobhan asked.

Lila feared that if she told Siobhan about her nightmare, she would hesitate in sending her back and send someone else in her stead. And despite the dread and lingering unease in her belly, she was determined to go.

"Just a little nervous," she lied, forcing a smile.

Siobhan studied her for such a long moment

that Lila feared she would press, but instead she stepped forward and took both her hands in hers.

"You will do well. And remember, you can always use a Summoning spell to contact me if you need help. Now. Are you ready?"

Lila wasn't, but she nodded. Siobhan held her gaze before closing her eyes, murmuring the words of a Transport spell.

A tug of wind yanked at Lila's belly, and the world dissolved around her. She disliked Transport spells; they disoriented her. They were akin to hopping on a motorcycle that was going a thousand miles an hour. They were a bit like traveling through time, though time travel was far more disorienting. She suspected Siobhan had performed the spell to prepare her for the more arduous trip she'd soon take through centuries of time.

When the world faded back up around them, they were a half mile away from the fairy pools of Skye. The portal was located in one of the tucked away coves near the pools; it was how the legends and stories started forming about these waters. Little did the tourists, who came to visit the pools, know that there was a magical time portal nearby.

Stiuireadh could technically travel through time anywhere, but the magic around the portals, where their druid ancestors once worshipped, was powerful and helped in pulling the stiuireadh to the time in which they wanted to travel. This was her first time using this portal. She and Avery had used Tairseach, the portal in the midst of the Scottish Highlands, when they'd last traveled to the past.

At the thought of her sister, her stomach lurched with unease. This was her first time traveling to the past on her own. What if she ended up in the wrong time? What if she simply disappeared from the fabric of time altogether? Such occurrences weren't unheard of.

"Doubt is the most dangerous thing when performing magic," Siobhan said calmly, with that eerie ability of hers to sense what Lila was thinking. "You are a powerful stiuireadh, Lila. Remember that. No matter what."

Lila tried to let Siobhan's words settle in, to believe them. *You are a powerful stiuireadh. You can do this.*

Siobhan stood back with a patient smile, and Lila knew that it was time. She gave Siobhan one last nod, expelled a breath, and stepped forward toward the cove, murmuring the words of the Time Spinning spell that would draw her back through time.

"A 'toirt seachad uine, cluinn mo ghairm. A 'toirt seachad uine, cluinn m'iarraidh. Stiuirich mi gu sabhailte tro do shigle."

Swirling darkness surrounded her as the world disappeared, punctuated by the distant sounds of voices and other sounds she couldn't identify. It was like traveling solo on a rollercoaster in the dark—a rollercoaster that moved faster than the speed of light. She knew it was the threads of time tugging her back, back, back, through decades and centuries, past an infinite number of births, deaths, wars, famine, destruction, joy, sorrow . . . until she felt as if she was suspended aloft in midair, before some force sent her hurtling toward earth.

The darkness around her lifted as a pair of strong, muscular arms wrapped themselves around her.

Lila blinked, disorientation seizing her.

She was now in the center of an unfamiliar forest grove. She looked up at the owner of the muscular arms—and her breath hitched in her throat.

The man was square jawed with proud, aristocratic features—firm chin, high cheekbones, generous mouth. His hair was a deep, fiery red, long and wavy, and a beard dotted his strong jawline. His eyes were a clear sea green—verging on blue—framed by thick lashes. He was broad shouldered and muscular, holding her as if she weighed no more than a feather.

It was the man she'd seen in her dream. But her dream hadn't done his masculine beauty justice. The man was preternaturally gorgeous, and for a dizzying moment she wondered if she was still swirling through time and this moment—this gorgeous man—was a mere hallucination.

But the hallucination spoke. His deep, Scottish brogue caused a fiery heat to encircle her entire body, lighting every single one of her senses aflame.

"I take it ye're the stiuireadh from the future," he said, his sexy voice filled with a trace of amusement. "I'm Laird Gawen MacRaild."

CHAPTER 4

The lass had appeared out of nowhere.

He'd been waiting in the forest grove for only a brief time when she'd materialized, on the verge of collapsing into a heap on the ground. Instinct had driven him forward, and he'd caught her in his arms.

His gaze roamed over her lovely features, arousal spiraling in his belly. This was not the matronly lass he'd expected. Her hair was a deep umber, now flowing loose about her shoulders, having come loose from her braids. Startlingly blue eyes peered up at him from a heart-shaped face with a wide, kissable mouth, delicately arched brows, and rose-stained cheeks.

"I take it ye're the stiuireadh from the future," he said. "I'm Laird Gawen MacRaild."

He shifted her light weight in his arms, trying not to let his gaze linger on those desirable curves of hers.

"Can ye stand, lass?" he grunted, attempting to stymie the desire that coursed through his body.

Her lovely flush deepened, as if she'd just realized he was holding her in his arms. She gave him a hasty nod and he released her.

She adjusted her bodice, which had slipped to reveal a tantalizing glimpse of her breast, and a surge of heat went straight to his groin. He averted his gaze, taking a step back.

"Thank you," she said, "for—ah—catching me."

Her accent was odd, shaped by strange consonants and syllables; he'd never heard such an accent. Did everyone from her time sound this way? *No*, he decided. Her accent may be common where—when—she was from, but he suspected that the loveliness of her voice, with its soft silken tones that wrapped around him like a summer's breeze, was all her own.

"I'm Lila," she continued. She gave him a rueful smile, the smile making her already lovely features even more so.

Lila. He'd never heard such a name before; it was a fitting name for someone like her: a mystical witch from the future. A desirable witch. He forced away the thought and turned away from her, giving her a curt nod.

She did something odd then; she extended her hand. He studied it, uncertain as to what he was supposed to do. He took her hand, recalling something he'd heard one of his nobles tell him he'd seen at the courts in France. He lifted her hand to his mouth and kissed it.

Her skin was soft and smelled of something

foreign and sweet; his arousal spiked, and he had to clench his jaw against the force of it. Christ, what was happening to him? Had she issued some enchantment to make him feel like a besotted fool when he'd only just met her?

"My horse is through that clearing," he muttered, abruptly dropping her hand. "Let's get ye tae the castle."

He didn't look at her as she made her way to his side and trailed him, her sweet, honeyed scent filling his nostrils. Annoyance flared within him. Was everything about this witch enticing?

"How did you know where I'd be?" Lila asked.

"I received a letter from yer coven leader informing me ye'd arrive in this grove," he said, gesturing to the surrounding trees. "Druids used tae worship here long ago; 'tis where the stiuireadh arrive whenever they come tae this time. I didnae ken the exact spot ye'd arrive, I just happened tae see ye as ye—as ye appeared."

It was odd to talk about witches and magic as if this were commonplace, even though he'd known about the existence of such things since he was a lad.

She seemed satisfied by his answer, falling silent as they made their way to his horse. He thought about what more he could say to her before they arrived at the castle. When he usually greeted a traveler, he would ask how their travels had been: if they'd encountered bandits, bad weather, or had suffered ill health. What did you ask someone who'd just traveled through time?

"My castle isnae far from here," he said finally, turning to gesture her forward once he reached his horse.

He swallowed hard at the thought of riding back to the castle with her, those lush curves of hers pressed against his body. When he'd assumed the stiuireadh who'd arrive here would be a matronly, older woman, he'd thought nothing of riding back to the castle with her. It would be difficult to concentrate with Lila's body so close to his.

Ignoring his lustful thoughts, he took her soft hand in his as he helped her up onto his horse, trying not to let his hands linger on the alluring swell of her hips.

He mounted the horse behind Lila, reaching around her to grip the reins. He again had to grit his teeth as his arms brushed against the swell of her breasts, and he kicked the sides of his horse—a little too roughly—and they raced out of the grove.

The ride to the castle was mercifully brief; the feel of her soft body against his was tantalizing torture. As they approached the familiar structure of Carraig Castle, he heard her soft intake of breath as she took it in with awe, and pride stirred within him. Carraig Castle had started out as a fort to ward off invaders from the north, built on a craggy hillside that jutted out into the ocean. Now it loomed ahead like a proud behemoth, its stone, turreted towers arching toward the heavens.

They entered the courtyard where the stable boys, who eyed her appreciatively, rushed forward.

His glower made the young men avert their gazes as they dismounted, and he led her inside.

He saw the curious glances of the castle workers as he led her through the halls of the castle to her guest chamber. Only a handful of the clan nobles knew of the stiuireadh and the Pact. For everyone else, the cover story for Lila's presence was that she was an old friend of his family's visiting from England staying at the castle for a time as his honored guest.

Lila kept her head low, her cheeks going rosy at the attention leveled upon her. This baffled Gawen. As lovely as she was, wasn't she used to people gazing at her in her own time? *Unless she's wed tae a protective husband*, he thought, a sudden discomfort settling over him at the notion.

Once inside her spacious guest chamber, she took it in with wide eyes.

"This is all for me?" she breathed.

He couldn't stop the amused smile that curved his lips. Her awe and enthusiasm were genuine, and infectious.

"Aye," he said, and gestured to a table where he'd had a servant leave a meal of bread and stew.

"For ye," he said. "If ye're hungry. After yer —travels."

"Thank you," she said. "Your castle is lovely, Laird MacRaild."

"'Tis been in my family for many generations," he said, a pang piercing him as he thought of how his parents had taken such pride in the castle.

"In my time, castles are relics. They're filled with

so much life here," she said, moving over to the window where she peered out at the bustling grounds, her lovely eyes filled with delight.

He watched her for a long moment, enjoying the sight of her infectious awe. He had to make himself turn away from her, moving toward the grimoire he'd placed on a side table earlier that day. She was here for a specific task, and he was honor-bound to help her fulfill it, nothing more. He had to look past how bonnie she was.

Lila turned, approaching him as he handed it to her. She looked down at the grimoire with wide eyes, running her hands over the binding with reverence.

"This is an Arsa grimoire," she murmured, her tone infused with awe. "It's only located in the past—and it's a bit of a legend among witches in my time. It can't be transported through time; there are only a few of these that exist."

He gave her a jerky nod, barely hearing her words; the incandescence of her smile was distracting.

"One of the stiuireadh who sealed the Pact gave it to my great grandfather. 'Tis been in my family for generations, for use tae any stiuireadh who may need it. While ye're in this time, 'tis yers."

Lila continued to gaze down at the grimoire with the same reverence he'd seen the devout gaze upon prayer books. She finally tore her eyes away from it, focusing on him.

"Siobhan informed me in her letter that there may be an aingidh in this time—and on my lands," he said, shifting his gaze away from those stunning blue eyes of hers. "If this is so, I suspect she may be behind two murders that have recently taken place on my lands. I've had some of my men look intae the murders of the two men, Clinnen and Daimh. They believe they're the result of a cattle or land dispute. But I donnae think 'tis so. Clan MacRaild is a peaceful clan with little infighting, and we've nae feuded with another clan for some time. After ye've had time tae rest, I'll take ye tae the site of these murders on the morrow."

Lila bit her lip as the joy in her eyes faded. A torrent of emotions played across her face: uncertainty, fear, and then determination.

"Good," she said, giving him a wavering smile. "Thank you."

"I'll leave ye tae get settled. Ye have a personal maid who will tend tae ye while ye're here. Ye will join the feast tonight in the great hall; 'tis best if ye show yer face tae lessen the curiosity about ye. Yer maid will bathe ye and provide ye with gowns. If ye need anything, ye only need ask."

He started to head for the door, needing to be out of her distracting presence, but she called after him.

"Thank you, Laird MacRaild," she said. "For helping me. For helping—us."

Us. The stiuireadh. The witches who had refused to help him when he was at his most desperate. Resentment flared to life within him, and his jaw tightened.

"I honor the Pact only for my father," he said shortly, and left her chamber.

Once he was back in his chamber, he ordered a servant to bring him a strong cup of ale. It frustrated him beyond end how lovely Lila was, how her very presence disarmed him. He'd have to continually remind himself what she was, and that she was here to carry out a specific task before she was back in the time where she belonged.

CHAPTER 5

Lila slammed the Arsa grimoire shut, leaning back in her chair to rub her temples. It seemed like she'd been studying it for hours, but she still had difficulty with the various spells: all written in Latin, Gaelic, and other Celtic languages that she had difficulty deciphering, given her rusty grasp of such languages.

If Avery was here, she thought bitterly, *she wouldn't be struggling with these spells.* And Avery certainly wouldn't have let herself get distracted by the sexy Scottish laird who'd caught her in his arms as soon as she arrived.

Her face warmed at the memory of her instant arousal as her eyes locked with his—her accelerated heart rate, the dryness of her mouth, the moisture that crept between her thighs—all of which she knew had nothing to do with traveling through time and everything to do with Gawen. The last time she'd traveled to this time, she and Avery had stayed with an elderly man with a white beard who'd reminded her of Santa Claus. He was worlds apart from Gawen, who was the most handsome man she'd ever seen—in any time. How was she supposed to get a handle on her magic with his distracting, sexy presence?

You have to, she reminded herself. *You're here for a specific purpose, not to swoon over the hunky laird.*

She recalled Gawen's words about the murders on his lands. If the aingidh in this time had done that using her magic Lila should be able to detect it using a spell. She closed her eyes and took a deep breath before murmuring the words of a Locator spell.

"*Taispeain an medicine dorcha seo dom.*"

She sat still and waited for the familiar sensation of her magic flowing through her, that telltale hum of electricity that rippled beneath her skin, but there was . . . nothing. No pull at her senses, no heightened sense of awareness.

Lila gritted her teeth in frustration. She'd only just arrived; maybe she just needed time to settle in before using her magic.

She stood, moving to the window to look back out at the bustling courtyard. Carraig Castle was in ruins in the present day, a destination for tourists who had to use their imaginations to envision what an imposing and glorious fortress it must have been.

No matter how many times she traveled, it never ceased to amaze her that she was in another time, living and breathing among its inhabitants. As frustrated as she was with the limits of her powers, she'd never feel ungrateful for the gift of being able to see and experience different times, something that most people could never dream of.

"My lady?"

She turned to find a young, petite, dark-haired chambermaid standing there, holding a cumbersome wooden wash bin in one hand and several gowns in the other. Lila immediately hurried over to her, helping her lower the bucket to the floor. The girl's eyes widened in surprise as she stammered out a thank you.

"I'm tae serve as yer personal maid while ye're a guest of the laird. I need tae wash and prepare ye for tonight's feast," the young woman said.

Lila gave her a reluctant nod. It would be odd having someone bathe and dress her, but Madeline had drilled the rules of this time into her. She was under strict orders to not stand out too much to those who didn't know she was a stiuireadh—and that included allowing herself to be prodded and pampered the way highborn ladies of this time were.

But that didn't mean she couldn't be friendly.

"Thank you," Lila said, giving the maid a smile as she helped Lila out of her clothes. "What's your name?"

"I'm called Mysie, my lady," Mysie replied, her voice so low it was barely above a whisper.

"How long have you been working at the castle?" Lila asked, as Mysie doused a cloth into the wash bin and began to rub it along her bare skin.

"Since I was a wee lass, my lady," Mysie said. "My mother brought me here when she found work as a kitchen maid; I never kent who my father was. She died of the same illness that killed the laird's family."

Lila stiffened at her words, surprise filling her. Gawen's entire family had died of illness? Siobhan hadn't mentioned this, but she hadn't told her much about Gawen, other than he was bound to honor the Pact.

Sympathy rose within her. Even though she often felt like an outsider for being the weakest witch in her family, she loved her parents and her sister; it would shatter her if she lost them.

"I'm sorry about your mother," Lila said. Mysie momentarily stilled, sadness flickering across her face.

"The laird was kind tae me, allowing me tae stay on after she passed. Most other lairds would have dismissed me, but not Laird MacRaild. He even allowed me time tae grieve before I resumed my duties."

Mysie dried Lila off with another cloth, her gaze trailing over her skin as she helped her into a fresh underdress and an emerald-green gown.

"Forgive me, my lady, but I've never seen skin as smooth as yers. Have ye never taken ill?"

"I've been fortunate to never fall ill," Lila said, aware that skin like hers was a rarity in a time before modern medicine.

To her relief, Mysie didn't press, braiding Lila's hair into the double bun style of the time, entwining each braid with white ribbons. When

Mysie had finished, Lila eyed herself in the mirror. She looked like a proper fourteenth-century, Scottish noble woman and nothing like a time-traveling witch.

She thanked Mysie, who left her with a polite bow. Shortly after she left, there was a knock on the door. Assuming it was another servant here to escort her down to the great hall, she swung open the door to find Gawen standing there.

He'd changed into a different white tunic and belted plaid kilt, his hair shining a coppery hue beneath the candlelight of the corridor. He looked even more handsome than before, and a prickling awareness danced along her skin. Gawen's eyes swept briefly over her, something unreadable flaring in their depths before it was gone, replaced by a polite formality.

"I'm here tae escort ye tae the great hall," Gawen said after a brief pause. "Ye look . . . well."

"Thank you."

"If anyone asks—" Gawen said, extending his arm.

"I'm a friend of your family's—your mother's side—from England, here visiting the castle for a short time as your guest," Lila said, reciting the cover story Madeline had given her from memory.

Gawen nodded and led her down the corridor and winding staircase to the first floor. They entered the great hall, a cavernous room filled to the brim with long, narrow tables and dozens of guests, a large fireplace at the far end of the hall providing both light and warmth, the fragrance of roasted meats and vegetables wafting through the air. As Lila took it in with quiet awe, she realized that practically every eye in the hall fell on her.

Gawen led her to the head table, where she took the seat at his side. As she sat, she noticed a blonde woman who sat across the hall shooting daggers at Lila with her eyes. Lila quickly shifted her gaze away, wondering, with a twist of her stomach, if this woman was Gawen's mistress.

She tried to ignore the various eyes on her as she looked around. Though she'd been to this time before, she'd never attended a feast at a castle, and the grandness of it surprised her. There had to be at least two to three dozen guests in attendance, and there were at least half as many servants moving about the hall, refilling pitchers of ale and taking and replacing platters of food. The plate before her contained smoked herring and freshly baked bread paired with a sweet-smelling wine. Her stomach grumbled in appreciation at the sight of it.

"I take it feasting is done differently in yer time?" Gawen asked, his voice low and for her ears only.

She looked up; there was an amused twinkle in his eyes.

"Yes," she said, thinking of the solitary meals she had in her studio apartment back in North Carolina, or the quiet meals she shared with Avery and her parents. "We only have large feasts like these for special occasions—holidays, weddings."

"I cannae fathom that. Feasting is commonplace at Carraig Castle," he said, looking mildly horrified.

"Not everyone has a castle, Laird MacRaild," Lila

returned, her lips twitching with amusement of her own.

Gawen returned her smile. The smile lit up his handsome face, making his green eyes practically sparkle; a rush of warmth rippled through her at the sight.

"Ye can call me Gawen," he said. "I insist."

"Gawen," she said, as if tasting the name on her lips. His gaze briefly lowered to her mouth as she spoke, before he averted it.

The man seated at his other side drew him into conversation, and relief skittered through her as he turned his focus to the man. The way he'd been looking at her had made it difficult to breathe.

Lila surveyed the great hall, wondering if the aingidh she sought was already in her midst. Could she be one of these unassuming-looking guests, using a glamour to disguise herself? But other than the curious, and mildly suspicious glances cast her way, no one seemed to bear any malice toward her. Well, no one except for the blonde who'd been glaring at her ever since she'd entered the great hall with Gawen.

Gawen spoke to her sparingly for the rest of the feast, introducing her to several other nobles and his steward, Aonghus, a tall, dark-haired man with kind brown eyes, who sat at their table. She didn't know if any of them knew who she truly was, but they all gave her lingering looks.

When the feast came to an end and everyone began to drift out of the hall, Gawen escorted her to her chamber.

"We ride out at first light tomorrow, tae the sites of the two murders," he said, when they reached her chamber. "It will be a ride of some distance; we will have tae stay at an inn. How long do ye think it will take ye tae perform yer magic and locate the aingidh?"

"It's not that simple," she hedged. "I don't know which spells will work; she may have cloaked herself. I've already tried to locate her, as has my coven leader."

His brows knitted together in a scowl.

"I thought ye could carry out yer spell, end this dark witch, and be on yer way. I donnae like kenning there are witches on my lands."

She stiffened, defensive anger swelling in her chest.

"I am nothing like the dark witch. I'm here to help; she's here to wreak havoc. The stiuireadh only want to protect the flow of time, to help people."

The smile Gawen gave her was edged with bitterness.

"I think the stiuireadh serve their own purpose, same as anyone," he bit out. "'Tis not natural tae travel through time. I'm assisting ye only because I'm honor bound tae do so."

"Speaking as a stiuireadh, I assure you I only want to help protect time," Lila snapped. "I want to stop her. We're not enemies, Gawen."

But his green eyes still burned with anger. He took a step closer, and despite her irritation, a current of desire swept over her.

"What is it that makes you distrust us?" she

asked, forcing herself to speak, struggling not to let his proximity distract her.

He stared down at her, his square jaw clenched. He was standing so close that she could smell the sweet wine on his breath and see the faint flecks of blue in his eyes. Her breath hitched; despite their mutual anger, there was no denying the flame of desire that had roared to life between them. Lila's simmering anger vanished, overtaken by desire, and she leaned ever so slightly forward, wanting nothing more than for him to seize her lips with his . . .

But he took a jerky step back from her, swallowing hard, his Adam's apple bobbing in his throat.

"Ye should sleep. I'll have yer maid wake ye tae help ye get dressed," he said, before turning on his heel and disappearing down the corridor, leaving her trembling with remnant anger—and desire.

CHAPTER 6

*G*awen gripped the reins of his horse, keeping his focus on the winding dirt road ahead as Lila rode along beside him. It had been exceedingly difficult to sleep last night, the memory of how close he'd come to kissing her searing itself into his mind.

She's a stiuireadh, he'd had to repeatedly remind himself. *A lass with the unnatural power tae move through time. A witch who can manipulate fate and destiny.*

Anger seized him at the memory of his family's suffering before they died, and the stiuireadh's refusal to help him prevent it. He tightened his grip on the reins. He needed to remain focused. Never mind that she looked even lovelier today in a gown of deep blue that emphasized her beautiful eyes, with strands of brunette waves falling loose from her braids as she rode, fanning around her face.

He forced his gaze away from her, returning it to

the road ahead as they made their way through the countryside dotted with rolling, green hills. Dampness hung in the air, potent with the promise of rain. Fortunately, the weather held during their ride, and they soon arrived at the outskirts of a small village on the edge of his lands.

As they approached the thatch-roofed cottage, the home of Clinnen and Vika Moray, he dismounted, turning to face Lila.

"Clinnen Moray's widow is still grieving," he said, giving her a sharp look. "If she doesnae want tae talk tae us—"

"Of course," Lila interrupted, glowering at him. "I have no intention of making the poor woman suffer."

He wanted to retort that stiuireadh rarely seemed to consider the feelings of others, but given the mutinous expression on her face, he held his tongue.

They approached the cottage as Vika Moray swung open the door, her brown eyes widening in surprise at the sight of Gawen.

"Laird MacRaild," Vika said. "I wasnae expecting yer visit."

"I apologize for taking ye by surprise. How are ye, Vika?" he asked, with a gentle smile. "Did ye receive the bread and meats I sent over?"

He'd known Vika and Clinnen Moray since he was a lad and would visit the surrounding lands with his father and steward to collect rents. His father had told him it was important to know the common folk who tended their lands. *These are the men and women ye protect, who swear fealty tae ye for this protection. Ye will only earn their true loyalty with kindness and equanimity.*

"I did. I thank ye, my laird. It will help me get through the winter without—" Her voice wavered, and she swallowed, her eyes briefly shadowing with grief. "Is there anything I can do for ye while ye're here?" she continued, her eyes straying to Lila with curiosity.

"This is Lila, a friend of my family's, visiting from England," he said. "She accompanied me on my ride through the countryside today. I wanted tae see how ye were faring while I was out this way. I want ye tae ken I'm still determined tae find out what truly happened tae Clinnen."

Vika's eyes shimmered with tears, and she gave him a grateful nod.

"I thank ye, my laird."

"Do ye mind if I ask ye more about what happened that night? Lila doesnae have tae be present if ye donnae wish. And if ye donnae want tae—"

"No," Vika said firmly. "I want justice for my Clinnen. Please, ye're both welcome."

They entered her cottage, and she poured them two cups of water she'd collected from the nearby well as they sat at the table by the hearth in the cottage's main room.

"Clinnen would often go tae the tavern after a good day in the fields. This last time was no exception. I kent he'd be coming home late, so I went tae sleep. Had I kent what was tae come . . ." Her face twisted with grief, but she made herself continue. "When I awoke the next morning, he wasnae at my side like he usually is. I went out tae look for him, and when I found him . . . he was lying on the ground in the back. It looked as if he'd been struck from behind. There—there was a ragged slash across his chest. His eyes were still open, but he was gone."

She pressed a trembling hand to her mouth, tears streaming from her eyes.

"Clinnen didnae deserve such an end," Gawen said gently. "I will find out who did this. Ye have my word."

Vika offered him a shaky nod, but her expression was still grief stricken.

"I'm sorry for your loss," Lila said, and Vika blinked in surprise; he couldn't tell if it was from the strange sound of Lila's accent, or if she'd been so wrapped up in her grief that she'd forgotten Lila was there. "I know it's not my place to ask, but is there anything else you can remember? Was anything missing from his person when you found him?"

Vika paled, and he shot a glare at Lila, but her gaze was fixed on Vika's face. Vika bit her lip, getting to her feet and disappearing into a back room before emerging once more, holding a faded bronze brooch.

"He always wore two of these. One belonged tae his grandfather, the other his grandmother. The one that belonged tae his grandfather is missing. I told yer men about it, my laird. They assumed the person who murdered him took it. But I donnae understand why a thief would only take one. Or why they would murder him for it."

At his side, Lila had gone still, her eyes trained on the brooch as Vika handed it to her.

"If this will help ye find out what happened tae my Clinnen—" Vika began.

"We can't take this from you," Lila said. "Is there something else—"

"I trust Laird MacRaild. I ken ye'll return it," Vika said, her eyes settling briefly on Gawen. The grief in her eyes dissipated, replaced by a flash of rage. "I want ye tae do what ye must tae find the person who did this."

When they left moments later, Lila remained silent, her expression contemplative. It was only when they were on their horses riding back to the inn that Lila told him what she intended to do with the brooch.

"I'm going to try several spells to see if I can learn anything about his murder," Lila said.

Gawen frowned, wondering how a spell could help her glean anything about his death. But he held his tongue. Though he knew of the existence of magic, he'd never understand how it truly worked.

Once they entered Lila's room back at the inn, he hovered by the closed door as she knelt on the floor, placing the brooch before her. She closed her eyes, murmuring the words of a spell beneath her breath. He couldn't help but feel transfixed as he watched her; he'd never seen a witch perform a spell. And Lila, as lovely as she was, looked even more so as her entire body seemed incandescent with the power of her magic.

She repeated the words of the spell several times before looking up at him.

"Nothing," she muttered. "I felt absolutely nothing. This aingidh—she cloaked herself well."

Frustration marred her lovely features as she got to her feet.

"Ye can try again," he urged.

"None of my spells may work," she said, expelling a sigh. "There's a dark witch in this time, killing the people of your clan—"

"We'll stop her. Together," he insisted. "Ye havenae eaten, lass. Perhaps ye need tae take a meal and restore yer body before yer . . . magic comes tae ye."

It was odd referring to "magic" as if it were a skill, akin to being a smith or a craftsman, but she looked mildly comforted by his words.

"What do you know about Clinnen Moray?" she asked, as they sat down to a meal of roasted pork and bread the innkeeper, a portly, older man by the name of Bhreac, had prepared for them in a private chamber. "Was there any reason someone would murder him? You mentioned your men think it may have been over a land dispute?"

"Clinnen never caused anyone trouble; he was a good man. I donnae agree with my men. As I mentioned before—land disputes are common. On my lands they've never come tae such a violent end."

Lila considered this, closing her eyes and rubbing her temples.

"Poor Vika," she said finally, opening her eyes. "You seem to know her well."

Aye," he said. "My—I was taught tae learn as much as I could about each and every person who dwells on my lands. For their fealty I protect them. 'Tis something I donnae take for granted. 'Tis something I intend tae pass down tae my sons."

She blinked at him, a startled look flickering across her face.

"I didn't realize you were married."

"Nae yet," he said. "Once I've done my duty and assisted ye, I intend tae marry and have heirs tae take over the lands of Clan MacRaild."

She cocked her head, studying him with an arched brow.

"What?" he grumbled, unnerved by her stare.

"You just described getting married and having children like it was a chore," she said, her lips twitching with amusement.

"'Tis my duty," he insisted, a swell of defensiveness rising within him.

"In my time, getting married and having children isn't a duty," she said, her eyes lighting up. "It's something to be cherished. To look forward to."

Was there someone in her time waiting for her? He would be surprised if there wasn't someone, as bonnie as she was. A foreign emotion rippled through him, one he didn't like. He forced down a mouthful of bread.

"Is there someone ye're betrothed tae? Or are ye already wed?"

"No," she said, and in spite of himself, relief

swept over him. "I've been too wrapped up in time travel and getting stronger with my magic. But one day I want to marry and have a whole soccer team of children."

"Soccer?" he asked with a frown.

"It's a—never mind," she said, with a light chuckle. "I just want a large family. Children I can pass along this wonderful ability to. But first . . . I need to prove to myself—to my family and my coven—that I'm worthy of it."

"Why do ye think ye're nae worthy?"

"If you met my sister—or any other member of my family—you'd understand. I'm by far the weakest. You just saw an example of my weakness," she said, shame filling her eyes.

"Lila, I saw ye appear out of thin air. Ye just traveled through centuries. That tae me is nae the act of a weak witch."

But Lila didn't look convinced as she got to her feet. She moved over to the window, looking out at the darkening sky.

"My sister would have found the dark witch by now," she said, envy flitting across her expression. "My parents, and the coven, would have been happy to send her here instead of me. I love my sister, but she's always been . . . *more* than me. More beautiful. More powerful."

"She cannae be more beautiful than you," he said without hesitation, the words tumbling from his lips before he could stop them.

Lila looked at him in surprise, a lovely blush staining her cheeks. He stood and approached, holding her gaze. He couldn't stop himself from reaching out to gently stroke her cheek. Her skin felt like silk beneath his fingers, and he wondered with a surge of arousal what the rest of her body felt like.

"Ye're verrae bonnie, Lila," he murmured. "Ye must ken that."

The moment between them held and stretched into a long, potent silence. His gaze dropped to her lips, the lips that had tempted him since he'd first laid eyes on her, and it was as if an invisible force propelled him forward, until he was reaching for her and claiming her mouth with his own.

Her mouth opened up to his and he tugged her close, relishing in the feel of her curves against him. She kept up with the urgency of his kiss as his tongue delved into the sweetness of her mouth, probing its depths. He could feel her nipples straining against his tunic, and he let out a low groan as he kissed her, pulling her more firmly against him, his arousal evident by the strain of his cock against his kilt. He kissed her as if he could never—would never—get enough of her, as if they were the only two people that existed in this world, and for a precious few moments, they were. Nothing else existed outside of her body against his, her mouth yielding to the demand of his kiss.

When he released her, they were both breathless. He swallowed hard, trying to form a coherent word, or at the very least an apology. But no words came; his heart still hammered against his chest, and desire still flooded every part of his body. *One kiss,* he thought in a daze, *wasnae enough. Will never be enough.* He took another step back, as if distance alone could ebb his desire for her.

"I bid ye good night," he whispered hastily, and turned to hurry out of the room, his body still pulsating with unrequited desire.

CHAPTER 7

"The home where the murder of Daimh Singleir took place isnae far from Vika's," Gawen said, barely looking at her as they headed out to the stables.

Lila nodded, trying not to let his distance affect her. It was just past first light the next morning, and she'd spent most of the previous night fantasizing about Gawen, a painful ache between her thighs, replaying their kiss over and over again in her mind. When she'd come down to the main room to meet him, her heart had hammered in nervous anticipation. But he'd only regarded her with stiff politeness, offering her a curt nod.

When they reached the stables, he didn't help her onto her horse, instead allowing the young stable boy to assist her as he fixed his gaze anywhere but on her. She suppressed the wave of hurt that threatened to swallow her; it was as if the kiss they'd shared had never happened and they were polite strangers who'd only just met. But she shouldn't be surprised, given how quickly he'd fled her room after kissing her.

Maybe it's for the best, she told herself. The kiss, as searing and passionate as it was, shouldn't have happened. She needed to focus on locating the dark witch.

They rode in silence due west until they reached another thatch-roofed cottage adjacent to a small patch of empty farmland. There was no sign of life anywhere; the cottage and surrounding land looked abandoned. Lila gave Gawen a questioning look.

"Daimh's murder devastated his family. They returned tae the Highlands. Tae the lands of his wife's clan," he said. He heaved a sigh, raking a hand through his hair. "I've nae been able tae get anyone tae settle here since. There are many who believe this land is cursed after what happened."

Lila dismounted, unease settling over her as she looked around. While she didn't know if this place was cursed per se, there was a sense of pervading ... darkness here. A sense of evil. Unable to stop the shudder that rippled through her, she tugged her cloak close around her body, though it wasn't the brisk morning air that gave her the chill.

"Where was his body found?" she asked, hoping that she could keep the quaver out of her voice. She just wanted to perform her spell and leave this place.

Gawen gestured for her to follow, leading her to

the rear of the cottage. Her sense of dread increased, and she swayed on her feet. Gawen turned to look at her, his face creasing with concern as he took in her pallor.

"Lila? Are ye unwell?"

She gave him a jerky nod, stepping forward. She just wanted to get this over with.

"His wife found him here," Gawen said after a long, lingering look of concern, gesturing to a patch of ground just behind the cottage. "There was a ragged slash across his chest, just like Clinnen's."

Lila made herself move to the spot, sinking down to her knees. She placed her trembling hands on the ground and closed her eyes, murmuring the words of a Locator spell.

"Taispeain an medicine dorcha seo dom..."

At first, there was no response to the command of her spell. The familiar swell of frustration rose in her gut, but she swallowed and repeated the words of the spell, over and over, until her sense of dread grew, overtaking her like the force of a tsunami.

In her mind's eye, she could hear the rush of whispers. A swell of fury and despair filled her, so great that she began to shake. There was only pain, only darkness, and a gnawing sense of rage. She wanted to destroy everything. She wanted to watch the world burn.

"Lila!"

It was Gawen's arms around her that made her return to the present. She lay crumpled on the ground, and Gawen was helping her up. When she met his concerned gaze, she realized that tears filled her eyes.

"I felt her," she whispered, still unable to shake that sense of overwhelming darkness. "The spell worked—but it didn't help me locate her. It made me *feel* her. She's furious, Gawen. Furious . . . powerful. And she's close."

∽

"There's someone we're looking for—kin of mine traveling through these parts from England. We fear she may have been set upon by bandits," Gawen told the Bhreac, the innkeeper. "Have ye seen anyone pass through here? Anyone foreign, with an accent?"

"Similar to mine?" Lila added, forcing herself to sound casual though her heart was racing, and icy dread crept along her skin.

They'd returned to the inn after determining they needed to ask Bhreac if he'd seen anyone strange. If a time-traveling witch from her time had been here, Bhreac must have noticed.

She and Gawen had barely spoken a word since her revelation back at the cottage, but she could tell her words chilled him. *As he should be,* Lila thought. Whoever this aingidh was, she'd only just begun her path of destruction. A shudder went through her as she recalled that fury, so potent she could almost taste it. What had happened to the witch to cause such rage?

"There was a man and a woman who passed

through a fortnight ago," Bhreac said, forcing her back to the present. "They stopped here for a meal but declined tae stay the night, even though there was a terrible storm. The man sounded like he was from here, or the Highlands. The lass hardly spoke, but her accent sounded similar."

Defeat settled over Lila. The two people he'd just described were likely just frugal travelers from the Highlands. And they weren't looking for two people; they were looking for one.

"Is there anything else ye can remember about them?" Gawen asked.

Bhreac looked hesitant, and Lila stiffened. There was something he wasn't telling them.

"Please," she said, hoping she didn't sound as desperate as she felt. "If there's anything . . ."

"I'm getting older, so my eyes may nae be truthful at times," Bhreac said, after a long stretch of silence. "But I did notice that, well, the lass seemed like an older woman when she first entered the inn. When she left, she seemed years younger, like a lass barely out of her youth."

Bhreac looked embarrassed at the confession, a faint flush staining his cheeks. The unease that swirled in Lila's gut increased, and she clenched her fists at her sides to quell her panic. Bhreac didn't realize that he'd seen the aging and de-aging that was common among certain stiuireadh who traveled through time, called *aosu tapa,* giving them the appearance of seeming much older—or younger—than their actual age, all in the space of minutes.

"I understand. Sometimes my eyes give me trouble," Gawen said lightly. "Do ye ken what direction they were heading? They may have at least seen the kin we're looking for."

Lila was grateful for Gawen's ability to banter while digging for information; he was better at investigating than she'd realized. Lila herself was too shell-shocked by the revelation that the stiuireadh she'd been looking for had been in this very inn not long before she had.

"They were heading east," Bhreac said. "I thought that was strange; there's nothing but cliffs and ocean east. The villages and yer castle are all in the other direction, unless they were heading south first, but I donnae ken why anyone would want to do that."

Gawen thanked Bhreac, and when they were alone in her room, she turned to face him, her heart a battering ram against her rib cage.

"That was her," she said. "The dark witch I'm looking for. I'm certain of it."

She explained the process of aosu tapa among certain stiuireadh. Gawen listened intently, his face growing pale.

"We need to follow their path," she said. "I need to know where she was heading."

"Aye, but that was a fortnight ago. 'Tis already falling dark; we cannae make our way east now. She could be anywhere on the island—if she's still here."

"She's here," Lila said, another shudder passing through her at the thought of that rage she'd felt. She closed her eyes as that sense of rage swelled, threatening to overtake her.

The feeling dissipated when she felt a firm grip on her shoulders. She looked up to find Gawen standing before her, his handsome face creased with concern.

"When I was a lad, I was afeared of storms. I'd hide beneath my bedclothes whenever I heard thunder; it seemed like the heavens above were opening. My father found me hiding beneath the bed during one storm; I feared he'd scold me for behaving like a frightened bairn. But instead he told me that even the bravest men had fears, and whenever the darkness came tae take hold, tae seek harbor in my thoughts. Any time a storm came after that, I'd think of the calm waters of a loch I liked tae visit, and the fear—the darkness—would vanish. Can ye do that, Lila? Seek a harbor in yer mind from this dark magic?"

Lila closed her eyes, thinking of a camping trip she and her family had taken to the mountains when she was a teenager. It was one of her favorite memories: the laughter of her parents in their tent, the brightness of the stars in the night sky, the soothing sound of the crackling fire they'd prepared. As the memory of it filled her mind, a calm settled over her, chasing the darkness away.

When she opened her eyes, he was studying her intently.

"That worked," she said. "Gawen ... thank you."

He nodded, his eyes locked on hers, the air between them taut with electricity. For a few fraught moments, she shamelessly hoped that he would kiss her again.

But he looked away from her, murmuring a hasty good night before leaving, and as disappointment pierced her, she realized that, even if only for a brief moment, Gawen had served as that safe harbor from the darkness.

CHAPTER 8

*E*arly the next morning, Gawen stood outside Lila's door, his heart hammering in his chest as if he were a lad attempting to court a lass he'd just met.

A torrent of conflicting emotions had roiled through him once he'd returned to his room the night before. He'd wanted to comfort her, to pull that haunting sadness from her eyes. But his desire for her had sprung to life, and he'd wanted nothing more than to kiss her, letting his lips trail down the long, delicate arch of her neck, where he would lower the bodice of her gown, and—

Lila swung open the door, forcing him from the erotic thoughts that swirled through his mind. Her eyes met his, startled, and he swallowed hard at the sight of her, looking especially bonnie in her dark-green traveling gown, her hair no longer in its customary braided buns but hanging loose about her shoulders.

"Good morning tae ye," he said gruffly. "Did ye sleep well?"

"Yes," she said, her tongue darting out to lick her dry lips, and he had to stymie the wave of desire that swept over him at the sight. "The nightmares weren't as horrible as I feared."

Sympathy replaced his desire as he searched her eyes. He didn't know what it was like to sense someone else's fury and pain, and he could only imagine the toll it must take on her. His disdain for the stiuireadh temporarily faded as he considered what a cross such magic must be to bear.

"We should get going," Lila said, moving past him. "There may still be time to pick up her trail."

They departed the inn and made their way on horseback toward the rocky bluffs and cliffs that dotted the eastern shores of the island, a chill coursing through him at the thought of this dark witch who harbored such rage. Panic tightened his gut at the thought of someone with such dark power on his lands. He thought of Aonghus, of his loyal nobles, and the people who dwelled on these lands. As laird and chieftain, it was up to him to keep them safe. She had already murdered at least two men on his lands; he couldn't allow her to harm anyone else. He had to force himself to put his desire for Lila aside to concentrate on finding her.

They didn't know exactly which way the dark witch and her mysterious companion had gone when they rode east, but they stopped at a stretch of rocky cliffs an hour's ride away from the inn for Lila to attempt a Locator spell.

Lila dismounted from her horse, and Gawen held the reins of both their horses as she moved toward the cliff's edge. She took a deep breath before sinking to her knees, holding out her hands as she murmured the words of a spell.

As he watched her, an emotion besides desire surged through him. Awe. She didn't seem to realize it, but she looked so powerful whenever she performed a spell. Now, her long, brunette hair whipped around her face in the breeze, her eyes closed and her voice quietly commanding as she issued the spell, even over the sounds of the breeze and the roaring sea.

Her brow began to crease with frustration as she repeated the words of the spell, snatches of which he recognized as Gaelic and some Latin, before she stopped, biting her lip as she gazed out at the sea.

"What is it?" he asked.

"It's the exact opposite of what I felt at the cottage. I feel nothing," she said. "She's cloaking herself, or my magic just isn't able to pick her up. Or we're way off from her path."

"Let's have a meal, and ye can try once more. Then we'll need tae head back," he added, gesturing at the damp earth. "It may soon rain again."

She continued to gaze out at the sea before grudgingly taking the reins of her horse and following him to a nearby cluster of trees. He spread out a cloak for them to sit down upon as he handed her the bread and fresh water the innkeeper had given them for the day's journey. Her expression lightened as she took the food.

He followed her gaze to their scenic surroundings: the dramatic cliffs that jutted into the sea, the violently churning waters, the surrounding emerald-green fields, the sky aflame with an array of color.

"A fourteenth-century picnic on the Isle of Skye," she said, her eyes twinkling. "I can't complain."

"A picnic?" he asked, his brow furrowing in confusion.

"It's the term for an outdoor meal in my time. It's an act of leisure. My parents used to take me and my sister for picnics almost every weekend during the summer when we were kids."

"An entire family of witches," he murmured, shaking his head in awe. It was hard to imagine an entire family possessing the power of time travel.

"Yes," she said, smiling as she took a bite of her bread. But it faded as she continued, "And I'm the weakest among them."

He frowned; she'd mentioned this before. He didn't like this lack of faith she had in her own power. If only she knew how fierce she looked when performing one of her spells.

"What is it they do in yer time?" he asked, deciding to change the subject; he wanted to see the joy return to her eyes. "Yer family?"

"My parents own an antique shop in North Carolina. It's where my ancestors emigrated to from Scotland centuries ago. My sister and I help with the business—well, mostly I do. Avery likes to spend much of her time traveling."

"North Carolina?" he echoed. He'd never heard of this country.

"North Carolina hasn't yet been discovered by Europeans, but it's about four thousand miles . . ." She stood, her skirts flowing about her as she pointed due west. "That way. People from Europe and other countries eventually settle there."

Amazement settled over him at the notion of lands not yet known, but he was also distracted by her beauty as she stood, the wind ruffling her skirts, giving him a tempting view of her bare legs.

"What is it like?" he asked, setting aside his arousal as she sat back down, tucking her knees beneath her. "North Carol?"

"North Carolina," she corrected, her mouth twitching with amusement. "It's beautiful. I didn't appreciate it when I was a teenager; I just wanted to get used to my magic and travel to different times and places. But now that I think about it, parts of it are just like Scotland. I can see how my ancestors saw it as an extension of their home."

She nibbled on her bread, drawing attention to those sensual lips of hers, and he looked away.

They ate in silence for several moments before she looked up with a soft gasp. He followed her gaze, a smile curving his lips. A rainbow arched over the sky in the distance.

"My parents used to tell me and my sister that rainbows were remnants of all of the spells witches have performed throughout the ages." Lila chuckled, amusement in her eyes. "I was naïve enough to believe them when I was a girl."

"My parents would tell us that rainbows were the work of the *sidhe*," he said, smiling at the memory of the stories they used to tell him and his sister before the nurses took them to bed.

Lila was looking at him with curiosity, and he realized she wanted him to tell her more. And for a moment, he was tempted to tell her more—the love his parents had shared, how he'd wanted a love like theirs when he was younger and hadn't yet experienced such a great loss, how his sister's eyes would light up every time she saw a rainbow, and she would grab his hand, racing out to the courtyard so they could take it in together.

But then he recalled their illness, the life draining from their eyes, and the refusal of Lila's kind, the stiuireadh, to help him prevent their suffering—their deaths.

He stiffened, getting to his feet and setting his jaw. *She is a stiuireadh here tae find a dark witch and expel her from yer lands. Yer people are in danger. That is yer only concern.*

"Do ye want tae try yer spell again before we return?" he asked, not looking at her.

"Yes," she said, after a brief pause.

Though he wasn't looking at her, he could hear the slight hurt in her tone from his abruptness. But he kept his gaze averted.

He followed her back to the bluff, where this time she moved along the edge, so close that it made him uneasy. She stopped abruptly, closing her eyes, her mouth murmuring the words of a spell.

She sank to her knees as she repeated the words

of the spell, raising her hands, and panic seized him when he saw that *blood* had begun to seep from her palms.

"Lila!" he shouted, racing forward.

She opened her eyes and looked down at her hands, shaking. He stumbled forward, using the cloak to wrap around her bleeding hands.

"Why are ye bleeding?" he demanded.

"I sensed . . . blood. Animal blood. So I used a Conjuring spell," she whispered, her face going pale. "There was a Sacrificial blood spell done somewhere near—by the aingidh. She sacrificed an animal to perform it."

He frowned, not understanding why Lila looked so shaken by this. The druids once used animal sacrifice in their rituals, and his father had told him that sometimes the stiuireadh still performed such a practice.

"Animal sacrifice is no longer done in my time by stiuireadh; it hasn't been for centuries," Lila said, answering his silent question. "I came here assuming the aingidh I'm looking for is also from the present—that's what my coven leader assumed as well. But if she's using animal sacrifice, she's likely not from my time. Gawen . . . I think the dark witch we're looking for is from the past."

CHAPTER 9

Lila was still reeling from her revelation when she and Gawen returned to the inn. She had even more questions now. If the aingidh wasn't from the present, what time period did she come from? The distant past to this present? Or another time period in the past to this time?

Before, locating the aingidh had seemed like finding a needle in a haystack, and that was with the assumed knowledge of what time she'd come from. Now that she didn't know which time line the dark witch originated from, it was akin to attempting to isolate a single granule of sand on a miles-long beach.

"I donnae ken all the details of yer magic," Gawen said, forcing her from her maelstrom of thoughts as they sat down to eat in the private dining chamber. "But how does the aingidh coming from a different time change things?"

"I've been using a certain set of spells from my

time to locate her, assuming she's from my time. But now that I don't know what time period she's from—I'm not certain which spells to use. And . . . this makes it harder to figure out exactly why she's here. If she was from my present, we'd have the same knowledge of this time. But now . . ." She trailed off, desperation roiling through her. How on earth was she supposed to find this aingidh?

"We can ask around this area. Perhaps someone else saw her and where she was heading," Gawen said, his brows knitted together with worry.

Lila considered this. They could do that, but it would take time. And that was the human, nonmagical way of doing things. She was a stiuireadh. She needed—*must*—use her magic.

"You can send your trusted men to carry out a search," she said. "But I'll use my magic—it's why I'm here."

Gawen studied her for a long moment, worry still lingering in his eyes. She wondered if it was worry for her or for his people, his lands. Given his abrupt distance earlier, she assumed none of his concern was for her, and this knowledge caused a shard of hurt to pierce her gut.

She stood, giving him a forced, polite smile.

"I need to think . . . to figure out how to proceed," she said, and left the room without waiting for his response.

Back in her room, she paced restlessly as the sky outside her window darkened, mulling over which spells she could use to find the aingidh and trying to guess what time period she'd come from. Another year in the Middle Ages? A distant time past—the Dark Ages? Or even earlier, to the time of the Celts?

She sank down onto her bed, recalling the dark dream she'd had before she traveled to the past, and the sense of darkness she'd felt at the scene of the Daimh Singleir's murder. She went still, her heart leaping into her throat.

Dread swirled through her veins, but she knew what she had to do.

～

Gawen swung open the door shortly after Lila knocked. She swallowed hard as she noticed that his tunic was halfway unbuttoned, and she glimpsed a swath of muscular torso beneath.

He arched a quizzical brow, and for a moment she forgot what she'd come here to say. Why did Gawen have to be so sexy?

"Lila?" he asked. "Are ye all right?"

Behind him, she could see that he'd tossed aside his bedclothes; he'd likely been about to undress and slide beneath the covers to sleep. Lila could see his perfect, muscular body in her mind's eye, slipping into bed.

"Darkness," she forced herself to say, shaking the erotic image from her mind.

"What?"

"The darkness I felt before. I've sensed it before, in my time, in my dreams," she said, making the conscious decision to not mention that she'd seen him in her dreams as well. "I think I need to hone in on that to locate her. I've been avoiding it, but I need to face it. Since I don't know which timeline she's coming from, I'm going to use the oldest Locator spell I know from that grimoire you gave me."

He nodded, but she could see the question in his eyes. *Magic is her responsibility. What is she coming to me for?*

She stepped inside his room, not wanting to risk being overheard. He closed the door and turned to face her, his brow creased.

"That darkness—it's hard to describe. It's like being sucked into the center of a storm, and it'll be difficult for me to get my bearings. I need your help to pull me out of it. Otherwise . . ." She trailed off, fear seizing her at the thought of being stuck in that darkness, that swirling rage and despair.

He stepped forward, taking her hands in his. Sparks of heat danced along her flesh from where he touched her; it was a feeling akin to her magic.

"Aye," he said gently. "I will do whatever I can tae help."

As their eyes locked, she suddenly ached for him to kiss her, to take away her fear and uncertainty, replacing it with that swirling desire.

But she made herself step back, moving to a chair in the corner of the room. She felt his eyes on her as she made herself comfortable.

"When do ye need me tae—"

"You'll know," she said, giving him a shaky smile. "If I start screaming, that's a good indication."

But he didn't chuckle or even smile at her jest. Instead, he gave her a concerned frown.

"Lila, are ye certain that—"

"I have to find her," she said. "This is the best way. It's what I'm here for."

She said this to remind him as much as to remind herself.

He still looked concerned but nodded, taking a seat on the bed, his worried eyes trained on her. She expelled a long, slow breath and closed her eyes, murmuring the words of an old spell from the Arsa grimoire that she'd memorized.

Spells changed subtly over time; a different command, a different word, a variance to the language. This Locator spell was different from the ones she'd practiced in her own time; she hoped it led her to the aingidh.

"Tha na feadhainn as sine a tha mi ag iarraidh a 'nochdadh an bhana-bhuidsich dorcha seo dhomh."

Lila held her breath after reciting the spell. She thought she would feel nothing for a while, that the familiar frustration would take hold, but the exact opposite happened.

Pulsating rage and grief flooded her, a fury so searing that it seemed to scorch her insides. And she knew with an utter certainty that she was *feeling* the dark witch—the witch always seemed to burn with fury. Her instinct was to jerk herself away from this rage, this feeling of darkness, but instead she allowed the dark emotions to consume her, and repeated the words of the spell.

More grief and despair. Blinding fury. Lila

couldn't see anything, only feel, that overwhelming darkness dominating her mind. She repeated the words of the spell, ignoring her instincts to flee from this sense of evil that had settled over her.

Through the darkness, she saw a glimpse of something. It was brief and hazy, appearing for only a millisecond in her mind's eye, but what she saw was unmistakable. It was Carraig Castle—Gawen's castle—looming in the distance. The sense of rage increased. Rage paired with pleasure.

"Lila. Come back tae me. Follow my voice."

The darkness ebbed, and Lila obliged, following the deep rumble of Gawen's voice out of the darkness, like a shining, gold thread in a sea of black.

When she opened her eyes, she'd somehow ended up on the floor, cradled in Gawen's lap as he stroked her hair. Concern filled his gaze as he looked down at her. She wanted to remain in his arms, to allow the warmth of them to comfort her, but she made herself sit up, her heart hammering as she recalled what she'd seen in her mind's eye.

"Gawen," she whispered, panic clawing its way through her chest, "I felt her. I *saw* her—and I know where she's going."

CHAPTER 10

"She's going to Carraig Castle. I saw it in my vision of her."

Panic seized Gawen at Lila's words. The thought of this aingidh at his castle, among his people . . .

He turned his gaze to the window, his breath quickening with rising anxiety. It was already night, and rain fell from the dark sky; they couldn't travel now. They had no choice but to leave at first light.

Lila had already extricated herself from his arms, hurrying over to the small bag that rested next to the bed.

"What are ye doing?"

"Did you hear what I said?" Lila demanded, turning to face him with panicked blue eyes. "She may be at Carraig Castle now. If we don't get there—"

He stood and approached, taking her hands in his.

"Do ye nae think I want tae get back there? But

'tis the middle of the night in a downpour; we cannae leave now. Before I left, I had my steward put more guards on the castle and warned him tae stay on guard. We will leave at first light."

Lila's gaze followed his to the window. Her shoulders sank, and she heaved a sigh.

"We never should have left the castle. If my magic was stronger, I could have foreseen this."

"Ye donnae ken that. Had we nae left the castle, ye may nae have had yer vision, and we wouldnae even ken for certain if the dark witch was here. Ye need tae sleep," he said, stepping back from her. "I will come fetch ye at first light."

She nodded, but he saw a glimmer of unease in her eyes.

"Lila?"

"I'm fine," she said, forcing a smile. "I'll see you in the morning."

"Does something still trouble ye?" he pressed. "Ye can tell me."

"Nightmares," she said, after a long pause. "I—after a spell like that, I'm terrified of what I'll see in my dreams." She flushed with embarrassment. "But—it's all right. I don't need much sleep. I just want to get back to the castle and see if—"

"Ye can stay here with me."

He made the offer without thinking, but as soon as he did, he realized that he wanted to stay with her. Lila's eyes widened with surprise, her gaze darting toward the bed.

"In the chair, of course," he hastily amended, though he couldn't stop the erotic image of lying entwined with her in that bed. "If it will help ye sleep."

"That's not necess—"

"'Tis no trouble," he insisted. "I only have one question for ye."

"What?" Lila asked, regarding him with wariness.

"Do ye snore?"

She blinked in astonishment before her mouth curved into an amused smile.

"No. Do you?"

"I've been told I donnae," he said, and instantly regretted his words as he realized the implication, that a lover had told him this. For some reason he couldn't fathom, he wanted her to know this wasn't the case.

"When I was a bairn, my father had an addition built ontae the castle where my chamber was. I briefly had tae share a chamber with my sister and our nurse. Gordana teased me about my snoring; she told me I sounded like a dying horse."

Lila laughed, the lingering tension in her body seeming to dissipate. He returned her smile, a much-needed sense of levity settling over him.

"Ah—I need to take off my gown before I get into bed. I'll sleep in my underdress," Lila said when her laughter subsided, a faint flush spreading across her face.

Hot arousal shot through him at her words as he imagined what she'd look like in her underdress; the curves of her body even more apparent. He gave her a gruff nod and turned to step outside of the room as she took off her gown, trying hard not to think about the sensuality of her body. His cock began to stir at the image that formed in his mind and he clenched his jaw, trying to think of the most unerotic images he could conjure: the servants taking out the chamber pots, a stable boy cleaning out manure from the stables, but even those thoughts did little to stymie his desire.

"All right," Lila said, after a few moments. "You can come back in."

When he entered the room again, he almost regretted offering to stay. He'd seen lasses in underdresses before—he'd seen them in far less—but the sight of Lila in her underdress was painfully seductive. There was the firm jut of her breasts beneath the gown, the luscious swell of her hips, her flowing hair loose about her shoulders, her lovely eyes filled with shyness as he took her in. She looked like a virginal bride on her wedding night, waiting for her husband to devour her.

Gawen tried to stop staring; told himself he should make up an excuse and go to another room. But his mind didn't want to obey, his gaze lingering on every part of her alluring body before he forced himself to speak.

"Well," he said, his voice sounding strained to his own ears, "ye should sleep. I'll sleep in the chair."

Lila frowned, her gaze straying to the small and uncomfortable looking chair in the room's corner.

"Gawen, you can sleep in the bed. I know you're an honorable man. Besides, I'm not a delicate, unwed maid from this time. I think I can handle being in bed with a man."

At her words, acrid jealousy seared his gut. Her implication was clear; she'd shared a bed with a man before. Perhaps more than one. Perhaps many. He didn't like the thought of that, and his jaw went tight.

Again, he considered telling her he'd sleep in another room. But he couldn't resist the temptation of feeling that body of hers in bed next to him, even if it was chaste. It may be the only chance he had to do so.

He gave her a hasty nod of agreement, trailing her to the bed, which now seemed entirely too small.

"Do you need to change?" Lila asked, slipping into bed, looking at him with curiosity. "I know there's no such thing as pajamas in this time, but—"

"Pajamas?"

"They're clothes people change into for sleep in my time."

"There are clothes people wear just tae sleep?" he asked, knitting his brows together. He couldn't imagine such a waste of fabric.

"Yes," Lila said, looking amused at his bafflement as he settled into bed next to her. "Clothes aren't made by hand in my time—at least, not en masse. Machines do the work. Clothes are easier to come by."

"Machines?"

"This conversation could go on forever," she said, with a light chuckle.

"Well, 'tis no need for such pajams."

"Pajamas," Lila gently corrected, her lips twisting with another amused smile.

"'Tis usually hot in the chambers of the castle; the servants leave the fires burning through the seasons. When 'tis not the dead of winter, I sleep in the nude."

A hot flush spread across her cheeks, and he couldn't stop the grin that spread across his face. Perhaps the lovely witch was more innocent than she seemed. A jolt of pure male delight rippled through him at the thought that she'd never lain in bed with a naked man before, though the idea was impossible, given how bonnie she was.

She laid her head down, and he had to resist the urge to brush a stray strand of hair from her face. Though he had bedded lasses before, it struck him that he'd never simply . . . lain with a lass. He'd not allowed any mistress he'd bedded to remain in his bed after lovemaking; it seemed too personal, too intimate. Instead, he'd have a trusted guard escort them back to their own guest chamber.

He studied Lila. Her eyes had become far away again as she stared up at the ceiling, and he saw that fear return to her eyes. She must have been thinking about the aingidh, or whatever she'd seen in her vision. He reached out to touch her face, turning her attention toward him.

"When we saw the rainbow earlier, it reminded me of how my mother would take me and Gordana out tae the courtyard tae watch one whenever they appeared. She told us that there was another meaning tae the rainbow—that no matter what darkness life would bring, there would always be light after. I tried tae remember those words after she died. But I confess . . . 'tis been difficult."

"That's similar to what my parents have always told me and Avery," Lila said, a nostalgic smile touching her lips. "They would tell us that our gift of magic can bring great light, or great darkness. That we would sometimes be forced to grapple with the darkness. But I've never experienced such darkness until now. Until I felt the dark witch. I know I'm the one who has to stop her, but . . . " She closed her eyes and shuddered. "I'm scared. And I hate being scared. I should be stronger; I should—"

"The bravest men experience fear. Donnae consider yer fear a weakness, lass. Consider it a strength. Consider it . . . a light tae combat the darkness."

"How can fear be a strength?"

"It means ye have something worth fighting for. Something worth defeating the darkness for. Yer fear shows yer determination. It shows yer bravery. Never forget that."

"I think you have too much faith in me," she muttered.

"And ye have tae little faith in yerself," he returned. He reached out to touch the side of her face, and her eyes returned to his. He wanted nothing more than to claim her lips with his own, but he knew his desire for her would overwhelm him, and he would find it impossible to not make love to her.

He withdrew his hand and instead took her hand in his, raising it to his lips.

"Now sleep, lass," he murmured. "I'll be at yer side tae help chase away the nightmares if they come."

He lowered her hand and started to withdraw his from her grip, but she held firm, closing her eyes, and he realized she intended to hold on to his hand as she slept.

He watched her drift off to sleep, and he felt something open up inside of his chest, as if a door that had been locked shut was slowly being pried open. The feeling both thrilled and frightened him. He shouldn't form an attachment to Lila, but when he drifted off to a deep sleep of his own, settling in next to the warmth of her body, he realized something. An attachment to Lila that went beyond desire had already taken hold of him.

CHAPTER 11

When Lila awoke, Gawen was still sleeping, sprawled on his back. He was even more gorgeous in sleep, with the early dawn sunlight illuminating his handsome profile: the stubbled square jaw, the generous mouth, the strands of hair which caught the light like miniature strands of fire. Tendrils of heat coiled around her, and she swallowed hard as she took him in.

Gawen stirred, and she quickly averted her gaze, not wanting him to catch her staring. He turned to face her, his green eyes blinking at her for several moments as if he'd forgotten how he'd gotten there. He abruptly sat up, climbing out of bed. She tried not to let his abrupt departure bruise her ego.

"Did ye sleep well, lass?" he asked gruffly, still not looking at her. "Any nightmares?"

"No," she said, giving him a grateful smile. "I slept well, thank you. I think our talk helped."

"I'm glad yer sleep fared well," he said, already walking to the door. "I'll wash up in yer room. We need tae head back tae the castle post haste."

She watched him hurry out. Lila bit her lip as she got dressed, trying to ignore her lingering hurt. She'd never spent a night in bed with any man before. They'd both been clothed and hadn't so much as kissed, but it had been the most intimate night she'd shared with anyone.

When she joined him at the stables moments later, he gave her a curt nod, barely waiting for her as he rode out. Irritation prickled at her chest; he was behaving just as he had after the kiss they'd shared.

He doesn't owe you anything, Lila told herself as her horse trotted after him. *Last night he was just being kind. It meant nothing significant.*

But the thought didn't stop the memory of their night together from swirling through her mind: the deep rumble of Gawen's laughter, his comforting words, his potent masculine scent of oak and sandalwood as he'd lain next to her.

By the time they reached the castle, she thought she'd feel nothing but anxiety, given that the aingidh may be here. But in spite of herself, a sliver of disappointment crawled down her spine at the knowledge that her alone time with Gawen had come to an end.

When they entered the castle's courtyard and handed their horses to the stable boys, Gawen dismounted and gave her another curt nod, murmuring that he would speak to her later.

He's laird, and his people are in danger, she told herself. She needed to keep reminding herself that their emotionally intimate night together had changed nothing—they both had duties to tend to.

Lila returned to her chamber, where Mysie helped her unpack and change out of her traveling gown. As soon as Mysie left, Lila moved to the Arsa grimoire and flipped through it, forcing thoughts of Gawen from her mind. She needed to find a more precise Locator spell, to see if she could isolate the witch's presence if she was here at the castle.

Forcing aside her traitorous thoughts of Gawen, she closed her eyes, and began to recite spells.

∼

"My lady?"

Lila stirred, blinking up at Mysie. She'd fallen asleep after putting away the grimoire, exhausted from performing so many spells in such a short space of time. She'd gone through dozens only to come up empty. Her parents had always told her and Avery that performing spells was mentally taxing, but Lila was desperate to determine if the dark witch was within the castle walls.

"'Tis time for the feast, or shall I tell the laird ye're tae weary from yer travels tae join?" Mysie asked.

Lila sat up to look out the window, realizing that it was already growing dark.

"No," she said, shaking her head as she stood, approaching the gown Mysie had laid out for her. If the aingidh was still in the castle, she'd done a fine job of cloaking herself. And if she was here, what was her goal? To murder someone else? What if her target was Gawen himself?

The fear that struck her at the thought momentarily rendered her still, and Mysie gave her a curious glance. If something happened to Gawen, she'd never forgive herself. Determination gripped her. As much as she'd wanted to only use magic, she needed to use other means of finding the dark witch. She would get to know the wives of the clan; gossip was a viable way of gleaning information. The coven historian had told her that gossip and rumor was a vital way that information spread in the time before cell phones and the internet.

As Mysie washed and dressed her, Lila studied her. Servants had to have an ear for the comings and goings within the castle. She bit her lip; she needed to be careful with how she phrased her next questions.

"Mysie, do you have any friends in the castle?" she asked, hoping that her tone sounded casual.

Mysie paused from her task of helping Lila into her gown, studying her for such a long moment that Lila shifted beneath her gaze.

"No, my lady," Mysie said finally. "I keep tae myself and do my work. Why do ye ask?"

"I'm just curious about what's been going on here in the castle," Lila said, trying to keep her tone light. "There was always something exciting happening in my household back in England. I've just been starved for gossip, I suppose."

Mysie gave her another disconcertingly long look before she finished helping her get dressed and leaving her with a polite nod.

Lila headed down to the great hall, wondering why Mysie had given her such a long, probing look. *You confused the poor girl,* she chided herself. *She's just trying to do her job, and you're digging for gossip.*

She entered the great hall, searching for Gawen. He was seated at the head table next to that blonde woman who'd glowered at her during her first feast here. She was leaning close to him, murmuring into his ear. The jealousy that seized Lila took her by surprise, and she swallowed hard.

Gawen looked up, his eyes briefly meeting hers across the hall. Something unreadable flared in them before he gave her yet another brief, but curt, nod of acknowledgment. The blonde woman at his side gave her a look of cold triumph.

Forcing her gaze away from them, she took a seat at the opposite end of the table. Whatever was going on between Gawen and the blonde was none of her business. But jealousy still gnawed at her gut as she focused on her meal of roasted venison and bread.

"The lass at Laird MacRaild's side is his former mistress, Achdara," the woman at her side murmured.

Lila looked up, startled. She hadn't noticed the person who sat beside her, an older woman with dark, graying hair and shrewd brown eyes that were trained intently on Lila.

"She's recently widowed; I've heard they will soon wed," the woman continued.

The jealousy in Lila's gut sharpened; it took great effort to keep her hand steady on her bread. She gave the woman a forced, polite smile.

"Then I'm glad for him. I'm Lila," she continued, putting down her bread. "I don't think we've been introduced."

"Inghean," Inghean replied, looking slightly disappointed, and Lila realized that Inghean had hoped for a more dramatic reaction at the news about Achdara and Gawen. Was her attraction for Gawen so plain? "Wife of Baloch," Inghean continued, gesturing toward a stout clan noble who stood at the opposite end of the hall, conversing with several other nobles.

Lila eyed her. She could already tell that Inghean was a gossip, precisely what she was looking for.

"I haven't had the chance to make the acquaintances of many women here," Lila said, hoping that Inghean would take the bait.

"I'd be happy tae make yer acquaintance," Inghean said, her eyes lighting up. "Ye should come tae my home on the morrow."

"I'd like that," Lila said, her heart picking up its pace. She could only pray that Inghean had some valuable gossip she could use—especially about any mysterious newcomers to the castle.

The musicians began to play, and the guests stood to dance. To her surprise, Gawen stood and approached her, to Achdara's visible dismay.

"Will ye honor me with a dance, my lady?" he asked.

A rush of delight coursed through Lila as she took his hand and stood, aware of everyone's curious eyes on them.

He led her to the center of the hall. Lila's pulse fluttered wildly at the base of her throat at the feel of Gawen's hand on hers. He began to lead her in a dance that Lila was thankfully familiar with thanks to the coven historian and her former visit to this time; the Basse dance.

"I'm sorry I've nae come tae see ye; I've been discussing what we've learned with my men. They've informed me that no one new has come tae the castle," he murmured.

"My spells still haven't worked, so I'm going to use one of the oldest means of information sharing—gossip," she said, with a subtle gesture toward Inghean, who was watching them with interest.

"Inghean trades gossip like a greedy merchant," he said wryly. "I donnae ken how much of what she speaks is truth. Take care as tae what ye believe from her lips."

"I will," she promised, returning his amused smile as a searing awareness spiraled in her belly.

"Ye dance well for a lass from a time nae yet come tae pass," he observed as they moved together.

"I've been to this time before. And the coven historian Madeline made certain I was familiar with dances of this time," she returned with a smile.

"How is dancing in yer time?" Gawen asked.

"Scandalous," Lila replied with a light chuckle.

"You would have a heart attack if you saw how young people danced in my time."

"How so?" he asked, his voice dropping low, and the deep timbre of his voice caused a multitude of sparks to dance along her skin.

"Dancers move closer together," she said, her mouth going dry. "With more . . . sensuality."

"Aye?" he asked, his stunning green eyes locking with hers, his voice becoming even huskier.

Everyone else in the great hall seemed to disappear around them as she took him in, the moment becoming suspended in time as her breath hitched in her throat, her eyes scouring his handsome face, aching for him to kiss her . . .

But the music changed, and the couples moved into a circle formation; they were forced to move apart.

Gawen blinked, stepping back from her with an abrupt nod. His curtain of politeness returned, and that fiery desire that had briefly flared to life between them was stamped out.

Lila fought back her disappointment, dutifully dancing with other couples in circle formation before the music changed again, and she excused herself from the great hall, aware of Gawen's eyes on her back as she left.

Once out in the corridor, she took several deep breaths, willing her raging heartbeat to calm. She needed to quell her desire for Gawen; if what Inghean said about him and Achdara were true, it would only cause her heartache. And even if there were no Achdara, her time here was for one purpose only.

With renewed resolve, she headed down the corridor, but froze at the feel of eyes on her. She whirled, scanning the dimly lit corridor. She was alone. Yet the feeling remained.

Someone had been watching her.

CHAPTER 12

Over the course of the next fortnight, Lila made several visits to Inghean's manor home, located not far from Carraig Castle. She learned that Inghean and her husband had several grown children who now lived on the mainland, and her husband spent much of his time at the castle with Gawen attending clan meetings and going on hunts while she tended to the household. Lila got the sense that Inghean was bored; her incorrigible gossip seemed to be the only bright spot filling up her days.

At first, Inghean asked her many probing questions about where she was from and her family, which Lila answered with ease; she'd already practiced her backstory with Madeline and was prepared for most of her questions. After Inghean seemed to accept her answers, she launched into rumor mongering and gossip, mostly about other nobles' wives and the affairs their husbands were carrying on.

Lila would feign intrigue, trying to figure out how to glean the information she truly wanted to know without appearing suspicious. But whenever she asked a probing question about any newcomers to the castle or the lands, Inghean replied that she'd not noticed any new arrivals.

In her chamber at the castle, she continued practicing her Locator spells, but it was as if a door had shut on whatever she'd sensed in the countryside; there was no sense of darkness, no awareness of the aingidh. She recalled the sensation she'd felt when leaving the great hall after her dance with Gawen, that unnerving knowledge that someone had been watching her. But she hadn't sensed anyone following or watching her since that moment, and her magic remained frustratingly unresponsive, causing her old insecurities about her lack of power to come racing back to the surface.

She wondered if her lingering, unrequited desire for Gawen was the reason her magic had seemingly dried up. After their dance during the feast, Gawen had returned to being a polite stranger; he hadn't shared another dance with her since, and when he sent for her to inquire about the progress she was making in finding the dark witch, Aonghus was always in his study with him. She got the feeling he didn't want to be alone with her, something that caused hurt to pierce her chest. She tried to tell herself that Gawen's distance didn't matter, but thoughts of him still occupied every corner of her mind.

When Lila went to visit Inghean on a drizzling Tuesday afternoon, she'd decided that she was making no progress with the gossip angle. Inghean's gossip was just that, gossip, and Lila ended up spending her entire visits fantasizing about Gawen. She was going to politely end her visits with Inghean and return her complete focus to her magic. Maybe there was some spell she hadn't yet uncovered.

But as soon as she sat down opposite Inghean, she barely got a word in edgewise as the older woman launched into her customary deluge of useless gossip.

"—And then there's that Coira. She's kept tae herself for as long as I can recall and refuses tae remarry. 'Tis nae natural. There are many who say she's a witch—I'm inclined tae believe them."

Lila, who usually half-paid attention to Inghean's ramblings, froze at these words.

"Did ye ken that Colin McDonald has taken yet another mistress?" Inghean continued, her entire focus on the piece of embroidery she was working on. "I ken that wives must turn a blind eye, but he doesnae even—"

"I'm sorry," Lila interrupted with a polite smile. "Who is this woman you speak of? The one who refuses to remarry?"

"Lady Coira Ardis, widow of Raibert Ardis," Inghean said, her nose wrinkling at the very mention of the woman's name. "She's lived on the edge of these lands for years. Her husband died some time ago, yet she's since turned down all offers tae remarry. She never comes tae the castle except tae attend the Yule feasts."

Lila leaned forward, feigning intrigue.

"People say she's a witch? Why?"

"Well, I donnae share the company of such a person," Inghean said, lowering her voice to a conspiratorial whisper, though they were the only two people in her drawing room. "But I hear she kens a great deal about stiuireadh, more so than anyone on the isle. She has tae be in her fiftieth year, yet she never seems tae age. And she's been seen heading tae the forest where the old druids used tae worship."

Lila's heart hammered as she listened. Inghean didn't know how close she was to describing an actual stiuireadh. But Siobhan would have told her if there was another stiuireadh on these lands in this time. Then again, if this stiuireadh wasn't practicing magic, Siobhan wouldn't be able to detect her presence here.

Lila endured the rest of the visit, eager to get back to the castle to ask Gawen about this Coira Ardis.

When she returned to the castle, she immediately sought him out. For the first time in days, he was alone in his study, and a heated awareness flared to life at the sight of him. He was leaning against a table, studying a piece of parchment, looking especially dashing in his white tunic and forest-green belted plaid kilt. When she entered, his green eyes took her in, and she felt tongue tied. For the millionth time, she inwardly railed at the unfairness of Gawen possessing such masculine beauty.

"Lila?" he asked, arching a brow, the sexy rumble of his voice pulling her out of her stupor.

"Coira Ardis," she finally managed to say. "What do you know about her?"

"She's a widow who's lived on these lands for years," Gawen replied with a frown. And then his frown disappeared, an understanding forming in his eyes. "And aye, I've heard rumors about her being a witch."

"Is she?" Lila pressed.

"Coira?" Gawen returned with a short laugh. "No. She's just a widow who likes tae keep tae herself. Inghean thinks that anyone who doesnae come tae regular feasts is a witch."

Lila's heart sank. She bit her lip and gave him a grudging nod.

"If it helps, I can take ye tae see her," Gawen continued, his expression softening. "Perhaps I'm wrong and she is indeed a stiuireadh."

Delight raced through her veins, and she realized it wasn't at the prospect of visiting this Coira; it was at the thought of spending time with Gawen.

"I take it yer spells havenae been able tae locate the aingidh?" Gawen asked.

There was no judgment in his tone, but Lila still felt shame coil around her.

"No," she said. "But I'll keep trying. There—

there's no need for you to accompany me tomorrow. I can visit her on my own."

"She'll be more receptive tae any questions ye have if I'm with ye. She doesnae take kindly tae strangers," Gawen replied. "We can ride out after I have my morning counsel with my nobles on the morrow."

"Thank you," she said, starting to leave, but he strode across the room to approach her.

"How—how have ye been faring?" he asked.

"Inghean hasn't proven as useful as I'd hoped," she replied. "And my magic is still—"

"I'm nae asking about yer magic or yer search for the aingidh. I want tae ken how *ye're* faring. Here in the castle. In—this time," Gawen pressed, his eyes searching hers.

Lila looked at him in surprise; he'd been nothing but distantly polite to her and hadn't seemed at all concerned with how she was faring on a personal level. He seemed to read her thoughts, giving her an apologetic smile.

"I apologize for nae asking ye before."

"You have duties to tend to. I understand," Lila said. "I've been well. I've been to this time before, so it hasn't been too difficult to adjust."

She'd thought she would miss the modern conveniences of her own time while she was here, but it had been surprisingly easy to adjust to this time. It didn't hurt that she got to live in a castle as an honored guest of the laird's with her own dedicated maid, which was far better than living in her tiny studio apartment back in her time.

"I'm glad tae hear," he said, his eyes still trained intently on her face, and she realized how close they stood together, and that they were completely alone. Heated awareness shifted into desire. She needed to leave, but her body was rooted to the spot, unable to take her eyes off his handsome features, admiring the way the firelight caused his coppery hair to glisten, the way his thick lashes framed those startlingly green eyes of his. He was even more beautiful up close.

"Lila," he rasped, his hands reaching out to frame her face. Her heart was battering against her rib cage as he pulled her closer, until his lips were on hers, and he was exploring her mouth with a soft, sexy growl.

His hands wrapped around her waist, yanking her against his muscular frame as her mouth opened beneath his. She wound her arms around his neck as her nipples brushed against his hard chest; she could feel his hard arousal against her belly. He tasted of ale and smelled of honey and sandalwood; she pressed herself closer as he continued to claim her mouth with his, needing—aching—for more of him, for this glorious buzz of desire to never fade.

"Ah—my laird."

Aonghus's voice behind them was like a bucket of cold water splashing onto them both, and they abruptly broke apart. Lila's face flamed as she gave Aonghus a hasty nod before practically running out of Gawen's study, her body still humming with desire.

THE NEXT DAY Lila and Gawen rode out to Coira's cottage. It was indeed on the edge of Gawen's lands, and it took some time to get there. Lila tried not to stare at Gawen as they rode, her body still inflamed by the memory of their kiss in his study. His eyes had burned on hers when they'd met at the stables and he'd bid her a good morning, but other than that heated look there was no overt mention of the passionate kiss they'd shared, something that Lila tried to not let disappoint her.

When they arrived at the quaint cottage, a woman with intelligent and warm brown eyes and dark wavy hair streaked with gray opened the door, looking pleasantly surprised at the sight of Gawen.

"Gawen," the woman said warmly. "'Tis lovely tae see ye. I wasnae expecting yer visit. Please, come in."

Lila momentarily stilled at the sound of the woman's accent; it was most definitely the Highland brogue, but it differed from the other accents she'd heard.

They trailed her inside to a large drawing room, where she sat them down and brought them cups of water and ale.

"Coira, this is Lila, a friend of my family's who's visiting me from England. She's searching for someone. We wanted tae see if ye ken anything of her," Gawen said.

Coira's eyes settled on her for an unnervingly

long moment before she smiled. Her next words sent a shiver down Lila's spine.

"I donnae think she's from England at all, my laird," Coira said calmly. She leaned forward, her eyes still intent on Lila's. "What year are ye from, my dear?"

CHAPTER 13

In the space that followed Coira's words, Gawen and Lila sat in frozen, stunned silence.

"I'm sorry for nae telling ye who I truly am, Gawen," Coira continued, not taking her eyes off Lila, who had gone pale. "But these are dangerous times tae admit ye're a witch."

Gawen shook his head in disbelief. His father had told him there were no stiuireadh dwelling on their lands. Perhaps he hadn't known. Coira and her husband, Raibert, had always been unassuming, staying out of clan conflicts and social matters other than to occasionally attend feasts at the castle.

"I come from the year 1920," Coira continued. "I came tae the Highlands in the year 1370; I wanted tae experience the past. I didnae expect tae fall in love. I wed a Highland noble and came with him when he relocated to Skye. We have two grown children who now live in Edinburgh."

"I take it yer husband kent?" he asked, thinking of Raibert, a kind man who'd served his father well.

"Aye. Please donnae be angered with him. He kept my secret tae keep me safe."

But Gawen could feel no anger toward her departed husband. His gaze slid to Lila; he now understood how it felt to want to protect your woman.

"Why didn't you leave and return to your time?" Lila asked. "After your husband died?"

"By the time my Raibert died, I'd lived here for over twenty years. I was a foolish girl of twenty when I left my own time; I came intae my womanhood here. 'Tis my home now," Coira said simply. "Why are ye here? Gawen says ye're looking for someone?"

Lila explained the anomaly her coven leader had detected, the dark witch on these lands, and the evil she'd sensed with her spells. Coira's face grew pale at her words.

"I've been trying to find her but so far . . . nothing. Most of my Locator spells haven't worked. I've resorted to gossip to see if anyone's noticed any strange newcomers. It's what brought me to you."

"Lady Inghean, I take it," Coira said, a look of bitter amusement flickering across her face. "That woman has disliked me ever since I refused a social visit with her years ago."

"Believe me, I understand. Inghean isn't a woman who takes social rejection well," Lila said wryly. She leaned forward, studying Coira with hope. "Have you sensed anything that could help me find this aingidh?"

"No. I'm afraid my magic isnae verrae strong. It took much of my power tae merely come tae this time. But I do have an old grimoire ye can look at. There may be spells in there that can help."

"I'm not very strong either," Lila admitted with a shaky laugh. "My coven may have made a mistake in sending me here."

Gawen frowned, starting to reassure Lila, but Coira was already speaking.

"I donnae think that's true," Coira said, arching a skeptical brow. "Do ye ken how I kent ye were a stiuireadh? I could sense yer power. I've only traveled through time once, and I had tae use the portal at Tairseach in the Highlands. I've nae practiced much magic since. But ye've been practicing yer magic since arriving here, I assume?" At Lila's nod, Coira continued, "Ye're more powerful than ye realize."

Lila didn't look convinced, but she gave her a polite nod. Gawen's frown deepened; he didn't like Lila's persistent self-doubt. Why couldn't she see how strong she was?

"I managed tae bring this with me through time," Coira said, getting to her feet and opening the drawer of a side table, removing a small grimoire that she handed to Lila. "But I've never had cause tae use it. I hope there's a spell in there that can help ye."

Lila thanked her as they both stood. Coira reached out to take Lila's hand, giving it a squeeze.

"I hope ye'll come visit me. I'm sure there are many tales we can share."

"I come from the twenty-first century," Lila said, as Coira's eyes went wide. "There is much I can tell you—I'd love to come visit. I think I'd enjoy visiting with you more than with Lady Inghean."

Coira and Lila shared an easy laugh before Coira turned to face Gawen.

"Gawen . . ." she began. He saw the unease in her eyes and knew what it meant.

"Ye have my word I willnae tell anyone who ye truly are," he reassured her.

"I thank ye," she said, the tension in her expression vanishing. "And Lila, I hope ye find her. I loathe witches who twist their power to carry out evil."

As they left the cottage, Gawen was still reeling at the realization that someone he'd known most of his life was a stiuireadh. Before he'd met Lila, he would have been furious at the notion of a stiuireadh living on his lands. But he knew Coira well; she was a good woman, as was Lila. His bitterness toward the stiuireadh still lingered, but he now knew two who didn't possess the manipulative cunning he'd assumed they'd all possessed, given their power to bend time to their will.

His gaze shifted to Lila, who still looked pale as she mounted her horse. He'd tried to keep a polite distance from her, but that hadn't quelled his desire. It seemed the more he tried to distance himself from her, the more he ached for her. He didn't have to accompany her to Coira's home; he'd fibbed about Coira's disposition toward strangers; she was welcoming and friendly to all. He'd just wanted to spend time with Lila; his attempt at distance be damned.

Fire blazed in his belly at the memory of their kiss the day before. If it wasn't for Aonghus's interruption, he didn't know if he could have stopped himself from taking her. And given the way she'd responded, he knew Lila would have happily indulged him.

A swell of lust washed over him. He tried not to let his gaze linger on the alluring swell of her hips or her taut breasts as they rode away from Coira's home. He'd assumed Coira's true identity would have consumed his thoughts during the ride back to the castle, but it was his traitorous desire for Lila that seized him instead. He had to force his gaze away from her as they rode, and by the time they returned to the castle his cock was painfully stiff against his kilt.

"I'm going to look over Coira's grimoire," Lila said politely, after the stable boys had fetched their horses and they made their way into the castle.

He gave her a gruff nod, watching the sway of her hips as she headed inside ahead of him. Frustration surged within his belly; he'd just learned there was another stiuireadh on his lands, and he still couldn't control his desire for Lila.

"Send word tae my nobles; I want tae go for a hunt on the morrow," he practically barked at a servant who approached him.

During the hunt he could keep his ears open and determine if there were any traitors among his men.

And a hunt could help clear his mind, giving him space from Lila's tempting presence, though he knew that nothing could truly stymie his need for her.

～

EARLY THE NEXT MORNING, Gawen rode out alongside Aonghus and a group of his men for the hunt. He took in each of his men, his gut lurching at the thought of any one of them betraying him. He prayed that he discovered nothing suspicious during this hunt.

He wondered how Lila was faring, if Coira's grimoire had helped her at all. He smiled at the thought of her murmuring her spells, her eyes closed, her sensual lips mouthing the words. She may doubt her abilities, but she didn't know how at home she looked whenever she performed her magic.

Gawen had to make himself set thoughts of Lila aside as they reached the dense forest where he and his men usually went to hunt. They tethered their horses and spread out in small groups to stalk the deer who roamed this forest.

"The bonnie lass who's visiting as yer guest—is she kin of yers? Has she a husband?" asked one of the men in his small group: Leith, a noble he'd known since he was a lad. Gawen found himself stiffening.

"She has no husband, aye, but she is under my protection," Gawen returned, his tone harsher than he intended. "She's only here for a short time until she returns tae England. Ye'll keep yer sights away from her, Leith."

Leith looked surprised at his ire but gave him a quick nod of assent. Gawen ignored Aonghus's perceptive gaze, focusing on the clearing ahead.

He tried to concentrate on the hunt, to stamp out his jealousy at the thought of not just Leith noticing Lila, but any man noticing her. She was bonnie, and he was a fool to think he was the only one who'd noticed. He ignored the burning heat in his chest. *Lila isnae yers*, he chided himself. *Ye have no right tae yer jealousy.*

But his simmering jealousy lingered for the rest of the hunt, and he snapped at Leith when his arrow failed to pierce a fleeing deer. Aonghus gave him a disapproving look and guilt flared in his gut. He'd apologize to Leith when they returned to the castle, but he'd make it plain that Leith needed to stay away from Lila.

As the hunt concluded and he and his group returned to their horses, he stilled as he overheard one of his men, Niven, speaking in low tones to a companion.

"He was supposed tae return from the Highlands days ago, yet no one's seen him. I went tae his home and he wasnae there."

"Who do ye speak of?" Gawen asked.

"My brother Sgaire," Niven replied, after a hesitant pause. "But he has a habit of enjoying brothels and ale. I assume he's been distracted and will soon return."

Unease slithered through Gawen. Sgaire was Niven's carefree younger brother who had a habit of imbibing too much drink at feasts. On more than one occasion he'd had him escorted out of the great hall. But Sgaire was harmless, or so he'd always assumed. He recalled the innkeeper, Bhreac, who'd told him and Lila about a man traveling with the aingidh. A chill coiled around his spine. Could the man have been Sgaire?

"I'll send one of my men tae where he was last seen in the Highlands," Gawen said, trying not to betray his unease.

"My laird, 'tis nae necessary. I shouldnae have mentioned—"

"The safety of every man in my clan is important," Gawen said, leveling Niven with a hard stare.

∽

Later, after he'd returned to the castle and had dinner alone in his chamber while he reviewed estate accounts he'd been neglecting, he sought out Lila to inform her of what he'd learned, though in truth he just wanted to see her.

He found her in her chamber, seated in the center of the floor, murmuring the words of a spell beneath her breath. Her long hair was free of its braids, hanging down past her shoulders, her skin incandescent even in the chamber's dim light. His gaze trailed down the long column of her throat to the delicious swell of her breasts. His cock stirred as a hot, aching need tore at his chest.

Lila's eyes flew open, her lips parting as she took him in with surprise. Just the sight of her parted, pink lips stirred his arousal, and he swallowed hard.

She scrambled to her feet, approaching him with a polite smile. Her scent teased his nostrils: rosewater and honey. It took everything in his power not to pull her close and breathe her in.

"Gawen?" she asked. "Is everything all right?"

No, he wanted to say. *I want ye tae the point of distraction.*

"I just learned that one of my men, Sgaire, may be missing," he forced himself to say, his voice sounding strained to his own ears.

He told her what he'd learned about Sgaire not returning from the Highlands, and her eyes widened.

"What if that's him?" Lila breathed. "The man the innkeeper saw with the dark witch?"

"I confess that I hope 'tis not so," he muttered. "Sgaire may be a drunken fool . . . but I donnae think he's a traitor."

"Can I go to his home? I may be able to pick up something if he is working with her."

"Aye," he said, his heart leaping at the thought of spending more time alone with Lila.

He knew that he should leave her be. He'd told her what he'd come here to say. But Leith's words returned to him—along with his jealousy.

"Have any of my men . . . bothered ye?"

"Bothered me?" Lila echoed.

"Aye," he bit out. "Made any words or flirtations that were . . . inappropriate."

"No, not at all," Lila said, giving him a reassuring smile. "I've gotten some odd looks about my accent, but everyone's been kind."

He gritted his teeth, wondering how "kind" his men had been. His burning jealousy must have been apparent because Lila frowned at him with concern.

"Gawen . . . are you sure you're all right?"

She stepped closer, and her enticing scent once again teased his nostrils. From his towering height above her, he could see the alluring swell of her breasts beneath her bodice.

"No," he rasped. "Ye donnae ken how lovely ye are, Lila. One of my men inquired about ye, and . . . I didnae like it."

A pretty flush rose to her cheeks, and she lowered her gaze.

"Well, you don't have to worry. I've just been focused on this," she said, turning to gesture toward the grimoire that rested on the floor behind her.

"Aye?" he asked, unable to stop himself from stepping forward, so that they were barely a hairbreadth apart. "And nothing else? Because I havenae been able tae focus on anything since ye arrived in that clearing."

He reached out, tracing the outline of her pink lips with his thumb. Lila stilled, an unmistakable desire filling her eyes as she raised them to meet his, and his control shattered.

He reached out to yank her close to his body, claiming her mouth in a searing kiss.

CHAPTER 14

Lila's heart thundered against her chest as Gawen kissed her, a rush of hot need searing her veins. She almost let out a cry of protest when he tore his lips away from hers, his green eyes heavy with desire.

"Lila," Gawen rasped. "Tell me tae stop."

Lila drew in a labored breath; there was a strained desperation in his voice, but there was also desire. Need. A need which matched her own. She was tired of battling her need for him.

Keeping her eyes locked on his, Lila murmured a spell beneath her breath, and the door shut behind them. Gawen stiffened with surprise, his gaze sweeping over her with wolfish intent as he understood her meaning in closing the door.

"Ye're wicked, lass," he whispered, before reclaiming her mouth with his.

Lila leaned into him, her hardening nipples

pressed against the solid muscle of his broad chest. She let out a startled cry as he suddenly lifted her in his arms, walking with her to the bed, his lips still melded with hers. She instinctively wrapped her legs around him, gasping at the feel of his hardness against her.

"'Tis all for ye, my Lila," Gawen whispered, peppering kisses along her jaw to the base of her throat, where he suckled at the space where her pulse hammered against her flesh.

She whimpered as he lowered her to the bed. Her eyes clashed with his, and her heart did a somersault in her chest at the look of sensual intent in his eyes. But beneath the heated anticipation that surged through her, unease bloomed. As much as she wanted him—*needed* him—he needed to know that she hadn't done this before.

He started to lower his mouth to hers, but she evaded it, swallowing hard.

"Gawen..."

He mistook her hesitance and stilled, guilt marring his handsome features.

"I'm sorry, Lila. I—" he began, starting to extricate himself from her, but she stopped him, wrapping her arms around his neck.

"No, it's not that," she said. "I want you, Gawen. Badly. It's just . . . I've never done this before."

He looked down at her with a frown, confusion flickering across his face.

"Back at the inn, ye implied that ye've lain in bed with a man before," he said slowly.

"That doesn't mean I've made love," Lila admitted, an embarrassed flush spreading across her face, lowering her gaze. Taking a woman's virginity was more momentous in this time. Would he not want her anymore?

Gawen reached out to tilt her head back to meet his eyes, and she swallowed hard at the fierce possessiveness in his gaze.

"Ye're a virgin?"

"That's usually what not making love before means," she said, trying to keep her tone light, though her heart was a battering ram against her rib cage.

Now that the confusion had vanished from Gawen's expression, he was looking at her as if she were delicious prey, and he was a tiger on the verge of striking. The look thrilled her, a sliver of delight coiling around her. His eyes gleamed with possession as he leaned down to again seize her lips with his.

"'Tis a gift ye're giving me, sweet Lila. I donnae intend tae take it lightly. I will take care nae tae hurt ye. I do confess, kenning that no other men have had ye before brings me great pleasure."

He sat her up, and with torturous slowness disrobed her of her gown and then her underdress, taking in every inch of her nude body with reverence.

"Ye're lovely, my sweet Lila. From every strand of yer hair," he whispered, reaching up to tangle several strands of hair around his fingers, "tae the arch of yer throat . . ." He leaned forward to suckle at her throat, the act causing sparks of awareness to flutter in her chest. "The swell of yer breasts . . ."

He peppered kisses down to her breasts, where he seized one aching nipple into his mouth, and then another, causing her to shudder with pleasure.

She was panting with need when he lifted his lips from her breasts, pressing kisses down the expanse of her abdomen until he reached the juncture between her thighs.

"And this," he whispered, his green eyes looking up at her from between her thighs. "Yer sweet quim."

Lila cried out as his mouth clamped onto her soaked center, laving and suckling at her with his tongue. Her toes curled and her back arched; not even her magic had evoked such a reaction within her, this feeling of a powerful electrical surge coursing throughout her entire body.

"Oh God," she rasped, as he continued to feast upon her, her hands clenching into fists at her sides. "Gawen . . ."

"Ye're so verrae sweet, my Lila," Gawen whispered between licks. "I donnae think I'll ever be able tae stop."

His words—and the sensations his tongue produced in her body—caused her back to arch and fireworks to explode throughout her as a powerful orgasm claimed her body. Gawen kept his mouth firmly clamped onto her center during the throes of her climax, holding firm even as her body stilled.

She looked down at him, her breathing labored as she came down from the high of her orgasm.

He stood, divesting himself of his tunic and kilt, looking like a Celtic god with his muscular torso, his gleaming fiery red hair, his intense green eyes that burned with lust. Her mouth went dry at the sight of his masculine beauty, her eyes taking in every part of his large, powerful body. As her eyes drifted down the hard length of him, desire paired with anxiety swirled through her.

"Donnae fret, lass," he murmured, reaching out to touch her face with tenderness, reading the mild panic in her eyes, "I promise I'll be gentle with ye."

He held her gaze, waiting for her nod of acquiescence, and only then did he kiss her again, settling his strong body over hers. A thrumming desire built up within her at the feel of him. Gawen trailed his lips down to her jaw, and then her breasts, until she was quivering again, on the verge of another release.

"Look at me, Lila," he said gently. She obliged, meeting his eyes as he entwined his hands with hers, continuing to hold his burning green gaze as he slowly sank inside her.

Lila gasped out at the sharp pain of his intrusion, and Gawen stilled, his face strained with effort as he leaned down to nibble at her lips, her throat. Lila trembled, her breath heaving, and soon . . . slowly . . . the pain faded, giving way to a sense of glorious *fullness* that she'd never felt before.

She began to writhe beneath him, wanting more of this glorious feeling, this beautiful ache. Gawen chuckled, leaning down to brand her mouth with a fierce, searing kiss.

"Patience, sweet Lila," he murmured, and then he began to thrust in and out of her, causing another wave of desire to wash over her. She gasped, winding her arms around his broad shoulders as his hips began to undulate, and he let out a low, sexy growl of pleasure.

Soon, there was only the feel of his sweat-slicked body against her own, his lips against her skin, his cock filling her with that amazing fullness. She wound her fingers in the silken strands of his fiery hair, the world dissolving around her as her pleasure built to a crescendo, and her body began to quake once more as a second climax roiled through her. Gawen let out a groan as he too began to shudder, holding her close as he emitted a guttural moan of pleasure.

As they both caught their breath, Gawen remained on top of her for several moments before extricating himself. He wrapped his arms around her and pulled her flush against him. She nestled her head into the crook of his neck, which smelled of his familiar scent of sandalwood.

"Are ye well, lass?" he asked, reaching out to stroke her hair, his voice still husky with desire.

"Yes," she whispered. "There was pain at first, but it didn't last for very long."

He sat up, pinning her with a puzzled gaze.

"I donnae understand," he said. "Ye're the bonniest lass I've ever seen. How do ye remain untouched? Are the men fools in yer time?"

Lila flushed at his compliment.

"I've had two casual boyfriends, but it never got

far with either of them. I've always been too focused on magic and time travel."

"I am glad ye're untouched," he murmured, something primal flaring in his eyes as he gave her a wolfish grin. "I've desired ye since I caught ye in my arms in that grove."

"Even though I'm a stiuireadh?"

Her tone was light and teasing, but Lila hadn't forgotten his bitterness toward the stiuireadh.

Gawen lowered his gaze, and Lila tensed. Had it been a mistake mentioning his distrust of her kind? But it was important to her that he trusted her, and she needed to know how he felt now.

"My distrust of the stiuireadh is paired with my grief over losing my family," he said, and a stab of disappointment pierced Lila; he used "distrust" in the present tense. "I wanted them brought back tae me. I confess I still do. Grief . . . 'tis become my constant companion since they died."

His expression darkened. She could sense him withdrawing from her, and she sat up, touching his face, as if willing him to stay with her.

"Tell me about them," she said gently. "If you want to."

She feared he'd refuse, that he'd dress and abruptly leave her chamber. Instead, his green eyes softened, and a smile touched his lips.

"Sometimes," he murmured, "I can still hear my father's voice laughing from down the hall. He was verrae jovial, and I could hear his laugh from anywhere in the castle."

"Let me hear it," Lila said, with an encouraging smile.

He looked bashful for a moment, a faint blush staining his cheeks that matched his red hair, making him even more handsome. He sat up and drew in a breath before letting out a loud, bellowing laugh that reverberated around the chamber. It was indeed an infectious laugh, and she laughed in return.

"Perhaps you've inherited your father's laugh," she said.

"I'd like tae inherit a great deal more than that. He was a good man, admired by all. He took care tae ken all the people of the clan, from the lowest peasant tae the highest noble. He taught me tae do the same."

"And your mother?"

Lila listened as he recounted tales of his mother, how she'd let him and his sister sit at her knee when they were bairns as she embroidered, telling them tales of old Celtic myths. He told her of the vivaciousness of Gordana, so named because his parents had thought she was a lad when his mother was pregnant, how she liked to make everyone around her laugh, having inherited their father's jovialness.

"Your sister reminds me of my sister, Avery," she said. "I was always the shy one; Avery was the life of the party. I love her dearly, but I've always envied her."

"Ye shouldnae. Ye're lovely and ye're powerful," he said, reaching out to stroke the side of her face. "Believe that, my Lila."

Warmth spread throughout her chest at the words "my Lila." He shifted, propping his head up on his hand as he studied her with intense focus.

"Tell me more about yer time," he said. "Do ye miss it?"

"Strangely, no," she said, surprised by her own admission. "There are modern conveniences in the future, of course, but . . ." She gestured to the massive chamber that surrounded them. "Living in a castle isn't half bad."

He shared her chuckle, his eyes following hers around the chamber.

"What about the other times ye've traveled tae? Have ye preferred any of them?"

"I thought the nineteen twenties were fun, but there's something about this particular time that I enjoy the most. When Avery and I traveled to this time before, I instantly took to it. There's a peacefulness—a serenity—that I haven't found in any other time. Especially here in the Highlands."

"I ken ye're only here for a short time," he said, causing an odd lurch of pain in her chest. "But I'm glad that ye enjoy it here the most."

He smiled at her, one of his rare, unguarded smiles that made his green eyes sparkle and his masculine beauty starker. But the sting of pain remained at the reminder of her temporary time here, of the still-unfinished task that loomed ahead of her.

She forced the thought—and the pain—aside, as he reached out to tangle his hands in her hair, his eyes darkening with lust.

"I want tae ask ye more about ye, about yer magic," he said, his voice husky with need. "What ye ken about the ancient druids, how many spells ye ken. But first . . ." He gave her a sexy smile, pulling her in close to claim her mouth with his. Lila moaned as he pressed her down, adjusting his large body so that he hovered above her. "But first, sweet Lila, I want tae again explore this sinful body of yers . . ."

~

A SHARP BANGING on the door interrupted the serene sleep Lila fell into after Gawen made love to her a second time, and they talked until fatigue claimed them, Gawen peppering her with questions about growing up in North Carolina and how it felt to perform certain spells.

Now, Lila sat up, tucking the sheets around her as Gawen stirred with a scowl. It was just barely past dawn, the sun only beginning to highlight the interior of the chamber.

"Gawen!"

Lila stiffened; it was Aonghus's voice, and he sounded as if he were on the verge of panic.

"Gawen, I ken ye're in there."

Gawen shot her a concerned glance before getting out of bed and shrugging into his long tunic. He crossed the chamber, swinging open the door.

If it weren't for the panic on Aonghus's face, Lila would have felt embarrassed at him finding her in bed with Gawen. But Aonghus didn't look surprised at all, his gaze only briefly straying to her before settling on Gawen.

"There's been another attack," he said grimly. "And I fear 'tis the work of the dark witch ye're looking for."

CHAPTER 15

"I was separated from my hunting party," said Kudan Munroe, a haunted look in his eyes. "I heard footsteps approaching. I thought it was one of my men."

Gawen sat at Kudan's bedside in one of the castle's guest bedchambers, where Kudan's hunting companions had brought him after the attack. Aonghus and Lila hovered behind him.

Gawen was relieved that Kudan had survived the attack; the castle healer had already tended to his injuries and wrapped his arm with cloth. Aonghus had informed Gawen that the attack had taken place during a hunt and was directed only at Kudan.

Kudan was the son of one of his father's now deceased friends, Ivor Munroe, and had never caused anyone trouble. He couldn't fathom why the witch had attacked him.

Gawen kept his eyes trained on Kudan, trying not to betray his fear and ignoring the gnawing guilt in his gut. While he'd lain entwined in bed with Lila, the aingidh had attacked one of his men.

"But . . . it wasnae any of the men from my hunting party. It was a lass. She told me she was called Malmuira; she looked at me with such fury. She lifted her hands, and . . ." Kudan trailed off, lowering his gaze, his face growing more pale.

"Ye can tell me," Gawen said gently, though dread swirled throughout his veins.

"She lifted her hands, and a fire began tae blaze in the clearing around me. It surrounded us both. I—I donnae ken how she did such a thing, how she—" Kudan stopped, taking a shuddering breath.

Icy fear clawed at Gawen's throat.

"What happened then?" Gawen pressed.

"The fire—it was on my arm. Burning my flesh," Kudan whispered, his hand drifting to his wrapped arm. "I—I was certain I would burn alive. I pleaded with her, begged her tae spare me. My words didnae seem tae affect her, until she looked—bewildered. I started tae scream; there was so much pain and then—it ended. The fire was gone, and so was she. She'd vanished." Kudan closed his eyes, taking another shuddering breath. "I—I think I've gone mad."

Gawen closed his eyes. No, he hadn't gone mad. He'd encountered the very witch they were looking for. This was Gawen's failure; he'd allowed another attack to take place on his lands.

"What did she look like? Malmuira?" Lila asked, stepping forward.

Gawen spared a glance at her, noticing the paleness of her face, and the guilt that shadowed her eyes. She must have been blaming herself for what happened, when he was the one to blame.

Kudan looked too dazed to question why Lila was here, or why she was asking him questions. He still looked lost in the dark memory, staring down at his hands as he answered.

"She was a wee lass. Barely reached my shoulder. Long black hair she wore loose, down tae her waist. Her eyes," he continued, his voice beginning to quaver, "they—they were unnatural. The color of silver or a gray stormy sky. There was death in those eyes."

Lila paled even further, and a chill spread through every part of Gawen's body. He leaned forward, making Kudan look at him.

"Did ye tell yer men what happened?"

"I didnae want them tae think I was mad," Kudan replied, shame flickering across his face. "I told them I slipped from consciousness and awoke tae my burning arm. We'd been drinking ale before. I think they just assumed I'd imbibed tae much and started a fire."

Relief swelled over Gawen; he didn't know if any of the nobles who knew about the stiuireadh were on the hunt with Kudan, but he didn't need knowledge of the witch to spread. It would only cause panic. There was a reason those who knew about the stiuireadh were sworn to secrecy.

He leaned back in his chair, rubbing his temples. He now had his trusted guards who did know about the dark witch scouring the area where she'd attacked Kudan, searching for anyone suspicious, though he doubted they would find her.

"Kudan, I want ye tae ken ye're nae mad," Gawen said. "I'll have a guard accompany ye back tae yer home after ye've had more time tae rest, but I need yer word that ye'll keep the truth of what happened tae yerself. I'm sure that rumors have already begun tae spread, but I'll handle the matter."

Surprise filled Kudan's expression, but he gave him a hasty nod.

"Aye," he said. "But, my laird, if I'm not mad . . ."

Gawen held Kudan's confused gaze for a long moment. Kudan had suffered near death at the hands of this aingidh; he deserved the truth. He turned to Aonghus and Lila, who both gave him nods.

"Aonghus will tell ye what ye saw," he said. "Ye take all the time ye need tae rest; I'll have the healer tend tae ye till ye're well. I'll visit with ye again later."

He stood, briefly resting his hand on Kudan's shoulder before leaving, trailed by Lila as Aonghus remained behind, closing the door behind him.

He and Lila didn't speak a word until they were back in his study. Lila still looked pale, and he wanted to reassure her. It was his job to protect the men of his clan; Kudan's attack was his fault and not hers. But before he could tell her this, Lila spoke up.

"I need to know everything you can tell me about Kudan Munroe. This aingidh, Malmuira, identified herself to him and attacked him for a reason—and she spared him for a reason."

"Kudan and his family have been part of Clan MacRaild for as long as I can remember. My father was friendly with his father, Ivor; Kudan and his cousin Struan even spent time at our castle when they were lads. Kudan's father died of the same illness that took my family; his mother died long ago in childbirth. Ivor mourned so deeply that he never remarried. No one has ever spoken ill of Kudan nor his father."

Lila considered his words before expelling a sigh. He could tell by her expression that his words hadn't helped.

"I need to go to the clearing where he was attacked," she said, her brow furrowed. "Maybe I can pick up her trail somehow."

He nodded his agreement, studying her. An apology sprang to his lips for last night; he should have contained his desire. Their lovemaking had distracted them both.

Yet a comforting warmth spread over him as he recalled how Lila had wanted to know more about him and the family he'd lost. None of the lasses he'd bedded before or considered courting, including Achdara, had expressed such interest in him or his family. Lila had held on to every word, allowing him to reminisce, and to his surprise, he didn't feel the sharp pain in his gut when he spoke of his departed family. There was the lingering grief, aye, the grief he'd suspected would always be there, but now when he spoke of his family it was only with affection and loving nostalgia.

And there was the softness of Lila's beautiful body, the innocence she'd gifted to him that had filled him with a primal sense of possession. Even now his cock stirred at the memory of her luscious body beneath his: her sweat-slicked skin, her panting moans, the sweetness of her quim.

He forced the images aside, opening his mouth to apologize, but Lila was already making her way to the door and he knew that now wasn't the time. A heaviness settled over him as he followed her out; their time together last night had been a brief, glorious respite from the darkness this Malmuira posed . . . a respite they couldn't risk enjoying again.

~

Unease trickled down Gawen's spine as he took in the clearing where Malmuira had attacked Kudan. There was still a scorched patch of earth where she'd surrounded Kudan with fire. Terror swirled through his chest at the knowledge that someone with this much dark power stalked his lands.

Lila didn't speak as they dismounted from their horses, but he saw her hands tremble as she moved to the patch of scorched earth, kneeling down. She pressed her hands to the ground, murmuring the words of a spell. She repeated the spell several times, and by the last utterance, she let out a low curse of frustration.

"I sensed nothing," Lila muttered. "She has to be cloaking herself; she must know that another witch is searching for her."

She closed her eyes, clambering to her feet. When she opened them once more, they shone with tears.

"Last night—it shouldn't have happened," she said. Her words were akin to what he'd wanted to say, but they still caused pain to tear at his chest. "You told me to tell you to stop. But I let my desire control me, instead of focusing on honing my magic. Maybe I would have been able to stop her if I'd been focused instead of—"

"No," he interjected. "I am laird and chieftain of these lands. What happened was no fault of yer own —it was on me. I came tae yer chamber; I kissed ye. I cannae say I regret what happened, but—"

"But it can't happen again," she said, not looking at him. Gawen's gut clenched, but he forced a nod of agreement.

"I need to send a letter to Siobhan," she said, still not looking at him as she approached her horse. He hurried forward to help her mount him, heat spreading through him as his hands grazed her hips, recalling how her bare hips had felt against his fingertips the night before. Her blue eyes locked with his, and he saw a flash of desire in her eyes before she looked away once more.

What happened last night cannae happen again, he reminded himself, turning to look at the scorched earth the dark witch had left behind.

He mounted his own horse, riding out of the

clearing with Lila ahead of him, ignoring the pain that seared his heart.

CHAPTER 16

Conflicting emotions swirled through Lila's chest as she entered her chamber; the lingering ache of desire, along with shame. Her night with Gawen had been everything she could have hoped for. Even now, her face warmed at the memory of their entwined bodies, the feel of him inside her and his lips on every inch of her skin. But her shame rose, shattering her memories. While she had indulged herself in her desire, Malmuira had almost killed someone else.

Malmuira. Lila shuddered at the name. The name of the dark witch who'd caused the anomaly in time, who had killed, who would kill again. She had cloaked her presence, making her impossible to detect.

Lila had asked Gawen for parchment, quill and ink when they'd returned to the castle, and Mysie soon entered her chamber with the writing materials, setting them down on the side table before leaving with a curious look.

She'd never written with quill and ink, regretting not practicing with Madeline when she'd had the chance. It took some time for her to write the missive to Siobhan, recalling everything she could about what Gawen had told her about Kudan and giving her Malmuira's name. She needed help from Siobhan, to determine if Kudan Munroe played any significant part in future events . . . or if she knew of Malmuira.

If Siobhan couldn't provide her with any information about Kudan's role in the future . . .

Lila's throat tightened at the possibility. She would have to tell Siobhan to send another stiuireadh to this time, someone stronger than her, someone capable of locating the elusive Malmuira and destroying her before she harmed—or killed—another person. Her conscience wouldn't allow someone else to come to harm on account of her lack of power. A sharp pain skittered through her at the thought of leaving Gawen behind, a pain she made herself ignore as she composed the letter.

Once she finished the letter and waited for the ink to dry, she placed her hands an inch above the parchment, murmuring the words of the spell Siobhan had taught her to send the letter through time.

"Snaithlean uine, cluinn mo ghairm. Snaithlean uine, cluinn mo tagradh. Treoraich an litir seo gu sabhailte tron t-slighe agad gu Siobhan, san Eilean Sgitheanach."

Once the letter shimmered and vanished

beneath her fingertips, she got to her feet. While she was here, there was someone she could confide in.

~

"I MAY HAVE to return to my time . . . to have my coven send back someone capable of tracking Malmuira down," Lila said, taking a sip of the warm broth Coira had prepared for her.

Lila sat opposite Coira in her drawing room. She knew that Coira, by her own admission, didn't possess much magical ability, but she was the only other person she could talk to here who'd traveled through time, and Lila needed to vent her frustrations to someone who could understand.

"I donnae ken this has much to do with power," Coira said. "How do ye ken that another witch willnae have the same trouble? Donnae place such pressure on yerself."

"I have to," Lila insisted. "I came here for a specific duty . . . and I'm failing at it. Miserably. I—I've gotten distracted."

"By someone?" Coira asked, a bemused smile curving her lips.

Lila shifted in her chair, her face growing warm at the knowing look Coira gave her.

"I noticed the way ye and Gawen were looking at each other," Coira continued.

A denial sprang to Lila's lips, but it was pointless. Witches were more perceptive than most.

"It doesn't matter," Lila said instead. "I didn't come here for any other reason but to—"

"Do ye think I came tae the past seeking love?" Coira returned, arching a brow. "I was supposed tae be in this time for a fortnight at the most. But as soon as I met my Raibert . . ." Her voice trailed off, grief darkening her expression for a long moment. "Nothing compared—has compared—tae the love I felt for him."

At the word "love," Lila stiffened, her heart performing a catapult in her chest. She cared for Gawen, and she'd never desired anyone the way she desired him . . . but love? That's not what this was. It was desire, pure and simple. She shook her head, as if to deny it to herself.

"I desire Gawen, and he desires me. That's all. You've seen the man," she said, forcing a lightness she didn't feel into her words.

"If ye say so," Coira said, but it was clear she didn't believe her, giving her a long, knowing look. "Why donnae ye tell me how the future that I left behind turned out?"

Lila was grateful for the change of subject and launched into a brief description of the future. The Second World War, the rise of technology, including a man being sent to the moon, which made Coira widen her eyes and press her hand to her mouth. When Lila was finished, she studied Coira with a wry smile.

"Now that I've told you of the future, do you regret leaving it behind?"

"No," Coira said, without an ounce of hesitation. "The life I had with my Raibert was worth leaving it all behind."

A surge of envy filled Lila at her utter certainty, even at the look of pained longing in her eyes. For a brief moment, she allowed herself to imagine a future with Gawen, sitting at his side during feasts, having more scenic picnics overlooking the sea, taking long horseback rides. A brood of red-haired children; Gawen chasing them around the courtyard while Lila looked on with a smile. The sudden, sharp longing that rose in her chest took her by surprise, and she had to close her eyes and expel a breath until the ache dissipated.

When she opened her eyes, Coira was again looking at her with a knowing intensity. Lila wondered, with momentary panic, if she'd read her thoughts. As far as she knew, witches didn't possess the power of mind reading, though they could be preternaturally empathetic.

"Thank you for listening," Lila said, suddenly feeling very exposed as she got to her feet. "I should get back."

Coira stood as well, approaching her and squeezing her hands.

"In all things, magic and love, 'tis best tae follow yer heart."

~

Tis best tae follow yer heart. Coira's words reverberated in her mind as Lila returned to the castle.

Her heart swelled as she thought of Gawen; those handsome features of his, the way his eyes danced with laughter when he let his guard down. A lump rose in her throat, one she quickly swallowed down.

A future with Gawen wasn't possible. She was the one who'd told him their night together could never be repeated. And even if there wasn't a rogue, murderous witch on his lands, Gawen had told her he intended to take a proper Scottish woman as a wife, not a time-traveling witch. And why was she even thinking of such things—who Gawen took as a wife was none of her concern. By the time that happened, she'd be back in her own time. Yet a shard of jealousy pierced her at the thought of this phantom bride.

She halted when she entered her chamber, her eyes widening in surprise. It was as if her thoughts about Gawen had conjured the man himself; he stood in the center of her chamber, looking achingly handsome in his white tunic and dark-blue belted plaid kilt, his coppery hair sexily tousled, as if he'd raked his hands through it a dozen times. A sizzling desire burned at her center at the very sight of him. Making love to him had done nothing to satisfy her need for him: if anything, it had only increased.

"I wanted tae see how ye were faring. I've addressed my men and told them that until we find this Malmuira, all recreational hunting is forbidden. I'm having extra guards patrol the castle and the surrounding lands. I've ordered all of my nobles tae let me ken if they see anything suspicious," Gawen said. "Where did ye go?"

"I went to see Coira for advice."

"Aye?" he asked. "What did she say?"

To follow my heart. Something I can't do when it comes to you, she thought.

"She's not well versed in magic, so she just reassured me," she said, pushing aside the thought. "Gawen," she continued, swallowing the lump that again arose in her throat, "I've sent a letter to Siobhan telling her about Kudan. If she has no information about why he was targeted, and I'm not making more progress soon . . . I'm going to ask her to send someone else in my stead. Someone stronger, who can detect and defeat Malmuira before she harms anyone else."

She watched him closely, and even though she'd told him they needed to keep their distance, a part of her wanted him to ask her to stay.

Gawen just stared at her in silence, a storm of conflict playing out over his handsome features before his expression shuttered.

"Let me ken when ye are certain of yer departure," he said gruffly, as hurt and disappointment rose in her chest. "I bid ye a good night."

He strode out of her chamber, and Lila sank down onto the bed with trembling legs, her stomach going tight as a realization struck her with the force of a nuclear bomb.

She did love Gawen. Coira had seen it before she had. She loved him, and soon she'd have to leave him behind forever.

CHAPTER 17

Gawen dutifully kept his distance from Lila over the next few days. Yet their distance had the same effect as to when he'd tried to stay away from her before; his need for her only grew. His chest clenched at the thought of her leaving and sending another stiuireadh in her place; he'd wanted to protest when she'd told him of her plan but made himself hold his tongue, reminding himself that they'd agreed to not be lovers anymore.

He would miss more than just Lila's presence in his bed. He'd miss her radiant smile and laughter, her fierce determination, her kindness.

A melancholy over her pending departure descended over him, threatening to swallow him whole—a sadness he hadn't felt since he'd lost his family. He made himself bury the sadness deep within, just as he had during the three years after his loss, focusing only on his duties.

He met with local farmers concerned about the recent murders and the attack on Kudan. For those who didn't know about the stiuireadh, rumors were rife, with many assuming that a rival clan was targeting Clan MacRaild. Gawen had to reassure peasants and nobles alike that no such thing was occurring, that the murders and the attack on Kudan were isolated occurrences. As he took in their concerned expressions, he wondered darkly if they were thinking of his father: if he would have done a better job of keeping the clan safe.

"No one is even considering that," Aonghus assured him, when Gawen voiced his fears aloud. "Rumors are rife, aye, but no one doubts yer leadership. Ye're a well-liked laird, just like yer father before ye. But we must stop this aingidh before she harms anyone else."

"Aye. I ken," Gawen returned.

Though he and Lila were keeping their distance from each other, he knew she was focusing on her spells, determined to locate Malmuira before she harmed anyone else. Gawen had all of his guards on high alert, patrolling the grounds around the castle after dark. Still, he felt as if he was just waiting for Malmuira to strike again. He hated this sense of helplessness.

"I'm taking Lila tae the house of Sgaire tae see what she can glean," he continued, rubbing his throbbing temple.

He'd intended to visit Sgaire's home with Lila after learning he was missing, but both their lovemaking, and the attack on Kudan, had sidetracked him. He'd sent one of his men to Sgaire's home to see if he'd returned, but he had not. Sgaire's brother, Niven, and the rest of his family were worried. Not wanting to disturb Lila, and trying to avoid being alone with her in her chamber, he'd instead sent a servant to inform her that they'd visit Sgaire's home on the morrow. In spite of himself, he couldn't help but feel delighted at the thought of spending alone time with her, however fleeting.

Aonghus grinned at Gawen's statement, looking relieved.

"What amuses ye?" Gawen asked.

"I'm glad ye're spending time with Lila," Aonghus said. "Ye've been rather unpleasant tae be around since ye've been keeping yer distance from her. Why have ye?"

"'Tis none of yer concern," Gawen said. "And I've been unpleasant because there's a dark witch harming—and murdering—the members of the clan, people I'm honor bound tae protect."

"I donnae think that's the only reason," Aonghus said, still grinning.

"Aonghus—" Gawen began, exasperated.

"I'll take my leave, my laird," Aonghus said, giving him an exaggerated bow. But he paused before departing. "Ye should ken . . . from what I've seen when I've glimpsed the lass, she misses ye as well."

Gawen tried not to stare at Lila—nor focus on Aonghus's words about her missing him—as they rode out to Sgaire's home the next morning. It didn't seem like she missed him when they met at the stables; she'd barely looked at him as they mounted their horses and rode out of the courtyard.

Lila wore her hair in one loose braid that wound its way down her back, a riding gown of deep crimson clinging to her curves, and a hot spiral of desire coiled through him at the memory of what she'd looked like beneath her clothes. It seemed as if his witch grew lovelier by the day, making it difficult to control his desire for her.

Fortunately, Sgaire's home wasn't far from the castle. They soon arrived, tying their horses up in the stable before approaching. A single guard he'd posted there to alert him in case of Sgaire's return stood by the front door, giving him a nod as they entered.

Gawen hung back as Lila headed down the long hallway, making her way to the rear of the home and entering the bedchamber.

He trailed her inside as she moved to the center of the chamber, closing her eyes for several moments. And then, to his surprise, she made her way to the bed, lying down in the center. A shameful roil of lust swept over him at the sight: the memory of her lying beneath him as he thrust into her causing his cock to stir.

Gawen averted his gaze, trying to think of

anything but the tantalizing vision of Lila on the bed, but it took a Herculean effort to ignore the sight. How he wanted to join her on the bed, to taste those lips, to whisper how much he missed her, how much he needed her—

Lila sat up with a sudden gasp, forcing him from the tumult of his lustful thoughts. Her eyes were wide, her skin pale, and she took several shuddering breaths. He hurried to her side, taking her hands in his.

"I—I saw him. Sgaire. He—"

A look of disgust darkened her face as she scrambled out of the bed.

"He was in bed with—with *her*. Malmuira. She's just as Kudan described—long, dark hair, gray eyes. I don't know how long ago it was. Sgaire is her lover. And wherever he is, they're working together."

∼

"I WANT every one of Sgaire's friends questioned, I want everyone he's ever associated with questioned. I even want his former mistresses questioned. And bring them all tae me after ye've questioned them," Gawen barked to the men he'd gathered in the great hall.

After Lila had revealed to him what she'd seen, they'd rushed back to the castle where he'd sent for his trusted nobles and guards who knew of the stiuireadh, informing them that Sgaire was working with Malmuira. Lila hovered behind him as he doled out orders, and at the urgency and authority in his tone, his men heeded his orders without question.

When they all left, Gawen leaned against the table, rubbing his temples; a throbbing headache had taken hold. How could this have happened? The men of Clan MacRaild had always been loyal. What reason would Sgaire have had to do such a thing? Was it Gawen's leadership that was at fault?

"You couldn't have known."

Lila's voice was close, wrapping around him like a soothing breeze. He opened his eyes to find her blue eyes trained on him with concern. He wanted desperately to take her in his arms, to allow her very presence to soothe him. And damn him, he wanted to make love to her again, to hold her close as he claimed her body with his. He wanted *her*— her laughter, her softness, her joy. Her.

But he tore his gaze away from her lovely face. Lila had been right. They needed to keep their distance. It was his selfish desire for her that had distracted him. Learning of Sgaire's betrayal was yet another blow.

From now on, he would only focus on what was important, on the leadership duties passed down to him from his father, and his father before him.

There was also a looming fear that had begun to stalk him. What if Lila came to harm at the hands of Malmuira? What if he lost her? Fear and grief constricted his heart at the thought. Their distance, as difficult as it was, needed to continue. Perhaps it was necessary to lessen his growing feelings for her.

He stood, forcing a coldness into his tone that he didn't feel.

"Leave me be," he said, turning away to avoid seeing the hurt in her eyes. "I need tae be alone."

CHAPTER 18

Lila returned to her chamber, hurt still piercing her at Gawen's cold dismissal. *It's what you wanted*, she reminded herself, blinking back a sting of tears. *We each have our duty.*

What she'd just learned about Sgaire was a step forward; she'd brought several items of his clothing back to perform Locator spells on. She should feel encouraged that she'd made some progress, not dejected. But she kept seeing the coldness in Gawen's eyes, the exact opposite of the warmth that had shone in them when he'd held her in his arms.

It was difficult, but she focused on performing several spells on Sgaire's personal items. If he was still working with Malmuira, the dark witch must have concealed his presence, because Lila's spells gave her no sense of his current whereabouts.

Lila remained in her chamber for the rest of the day, stubbornly performing spell after spell, determined to make some progress. She even took her dinner alone in her chamber; it would be too difficult to face Gawen.

But her spells proved fruitless, and her eyes were heavy with fatigue when she finally shut the grimoire and crawled into bed, falling into an exhausted sleep.

When she awoke the next morning, it took a long moment for her to notice the letter on her side table. Her heart picked up its pace at the sight.

Lila scrambled out of bed, nearly tripping on her underdress to grab the letter. It was from Siobhan, she'd used a special Transport spell to send the letter to Lila through time.

Lila's heart sped up even more as she read Siobhan's words; she pressed her hand to her mouth.

She was on her way out of the chamber before she'd even finished it.

∽

Moments later, Lila sat opposite Gawen in his chamber as he read the letter. He wore nothing but a long, loose tunic; Lila realized with a flare of awareness that he must have slept naked and hastily pulled it on when she'd knocked on his door. Every masculine contour of his body was apparent beneath the loose clothing; the broad shoulders, the muscular torso, and an ache swelled within her at the memory of the thick hardness of him, now shielded beneath the length of his tunic.

She tore her eyes from his body and made herself focus on his face; his intense green eyes as he read the letter. Several emotions played across his handsome features as he read: astonishment, disbelief, and awe.

When he lowered the letter, it was with shaking hands. A long silence stretched between them as she waited for him to speak.

"I ken ye're from a time that hasnae come tae pass," he said finally, shifting startled green eyes toward her. "But it truly doesnae settle until I read letters such as this."

Lila gave him a jerky nod, her gaze shifting to the letter in his hands. While Siobhan knew nothing of Malmuira, she had dug up monumental information on Kudan. Lila had already read it twice.

Two centuries from now, one of Kudan Munroe's descendants, Enraig Munroe, will organize one of the bloodiest massacres in Scottish history. It will become known as the Bloody Feast of Nelkirk, in which twelve members of Clan McCaullum will be murdered by their hosts at a feast. This must be why Malmuira targeted Kudan.

It was the answer Lila had been looking for ever since she'd arrived in this time—*why* Malmuira was here. And now she knew what time period she was actually from. She could only guess that someone important to her must have died in that massacre.

Lila felt a small, fleeting stab of empathy. Wanting to prevent such a tragedy was understandable. What she couldn't understand was killing innocents, begetting more death, more darkness. And for all the answers the letter had provided, Lila had even more questions now. If Kudan was the target, why had Malmuira killed those two farmers? Why had she spared Kudan?

"Who else is Kudan Munroe associated with?" Lila asked. "If Malmuira spared him, maybe she realized she made a mistake. Maybe she meant to target another family member of his. Is he married?"

"No," Gawen replied, "but we can speak with members of his family, and I'll put more guards on them."

"I want to speak to him again," Lila said. "We can't let him know what's going to happen, but we can find out what connections he may already have to this clan in the future—Clan McCaullum."

～

THEY ARRIVED at Kudan's home just after midday. A pretty, young woman with dirty-blonde hair and wide-set, blue eyes opened the door, surprise flitting across her face at the sight of Gawen.

"Laird MacRaild," she said. "Was Kudan expecting ye?"

"No," Gawen replied, giving her an apologetic smile. "I'm here tae see how he's faring, Ysenda. Lila has skills as a healer, and she wanted tae come as well."

He gestured to Lila; they'd decided this was the easiest way to explain Lila's presence.

Ysenda gave Lila a polite nod and stepped back to allow them to enter, her face flushing at Gawen's kind smile. Lila wondered with a rush of possessiveness if he had this effect on every woman he met. *Probably,* she thought with an inward sigh. The man was sexier than sin; she couldn't have been the only one who'd noticed.

Still blushing, Ysenda let them into a large bedchamber, where Kudan sat propped up in bed. A tall, stocky man stood at his bedside; Gawen introduced him as Struan, Kudan's cousin and Ysenda's husband, which took Lila by surprise; Struan seemed much older than Ysenda.

Kudan was still pale, his arm heavily secured with a cloth bandage, but he looked better than when they'd last seen him.

"How are ye faring, Kudan?" Gawen asked.

"My arm is still a wee sore, but the healer says 'tis healing well," Kudan replied. "I thank ye for checking on me, my laird."

"All men of my clan are my responsibility," Gawen replied. He slid a glance toward Ysenda and Struan, giving them a polite smile edged with authority. "If ye donnae mind, Lila and I wish tae speak tae Kudan in private."

Ysenda and Struan obliged, leaving the chamber with polite nods. As Ysenda left, Lila noticed that she cast Kudan a lingering look. When she noticed Lila looking at her, she averted her gaze. A tendril of unease coiled around Lila's spine, but she set the feeling aside as she joined Gawen at Kudan's bedside.

During the ride over, she'd given Gawen careful instructions as to what he could and could not say. Informing Kudan of future events that affected his family could result in him trying to change things, which would only cause a disastrous domino effect.

She watched, her heart hammering, as Gawen asked Kudan if he or any of his family members planned to leave the Isle of Skye.

At the question, Kudan stiffened, hesitating for a long moment.

"No," Kudan said, not looking at Gawen. "Skye is my home."

Kudan was a terrible liar. Gawen seemed to realize the same, holding his gaze.

"'Tis nae a crime if ye do," he said. "I'm just trying tae determine why ye were targeted."

There was another long pause, and Kudan swallowed hard.

"I donnae ken why," he said.

Lila studied Kudan, wondering what he was hiding, and if this was the key to figuring out why Malmuira had targeted him. Gawen expelled a sigh and stood.

"If there's anything ye wish tae inform me—anything that can help—ye ken where tae find me."

As they rode away from Kudan's home, frustration swelled within her. Kudan was hiding something from them, she was certain, but she didn't know how they'd get him to confess. And there was that lingering sense of unease about Ysenda. There was something . . . off about the woman, something that she couldn't place.

"Kudan is lying," Lila told him in a low voice, once they'd arrived back at the castle and made their way inside.

"Aye," Gawen agreed. "I'll have my men keep close watch on him."

"What do you know about Ysenda?" she pressed.

"She's the daughter of a Highland noble, recently wed tae Kudan's cousin Struan." He stopped as they reached the base of the winding stairs, frowning down at her. "Ye donnae think she has anything tae do with Malmuira?"

"No. I don't think so. But I . . . sensed something off about her—something that I can't quite place."

Another surge of frustration swelled. Witches tended to be perceptive; she should be better at determining what rankled her about Ysenda. Gawen seemed to read her thoughts, reaching out to take her hand. His touch caused her heart to do a somersault in her chest, and a sizzling heat scorched her skin.

"If Ysenda—and Kudan—are hiding something, we'll learn what it is," he said gently.

His hand lingered as his green eyes probed hers, an unmistakable need flaring in their depths. But he blinked, and the charged moment came to an end.

Gawen gave her a curt nod and ascended the stairs, leaving her behind with that ever-present need for him; a need she suspected would never dissipate.

CHAPTER 19

*R*emnant desire still lingered within Gawen as he entered his private study moments after leaving Lila. He was failing at all attempts to remain detached from her. Just the mere act of touching her hand had set his senses aflame. He sat down by the fireplace, taking a long swig of ale and ordering the hovering servant to send for Aonghus.

"I need ye tae put a man on Kudan; I think he's hiding something," he said moments later, after Aonghus entered his study.

"Ye think he's a traitor?" Aonghus asked in disbelief, raising his eyebrows. "He was injured by Malmuira."

"No," he said. "But there is something he's keeping from me. I need tae ken what it is."

Aonghus studied him with lingering curiosity but didn't press, leaving him with a nod to carry out his order. Gawen turned back to gaze into the flames that blazed in the fireplace. What could Kudan be hiding from him?

He distracted himself from disturbing thoughts of Kudan by meeting with his guards who were patrolling the lands and who'd searched the area after Kudan's attack; none had seen anything suspicious. Setting aside his frustration, he spent the rest of the day locked in his study, reviewing rent records and land deeds. By the time evening fell, his eyes stung from reading the stacks of parchment by firelight. He pushed aside the last piece of parchment, rubbing his eyes, anticipation filling him at the thought of seeing Lila at the feast.

When he entered the great hall, his eyes swept the room for Lila. He didn't see her, and to his annoyance Achdara immediately took the seat at his side. Lila entered moments later, going still at the sight of Achdara, but made her way to the far end of the table where she took a seat.

He forced himself to make polite conversation with both Achdara and the noble who sat at his other side during the feast, trying to keep his eyes off Lila. When the musicians began to play midway during the feast, another surge of annoyance coursed through him as Aonghus moved to Lila, murmuring something in her ear. She smiled, that smile that was both infectious and incandescent, taking Aonghus's hand and moving to the center of the hall.

Gawen clenched his jaw as he watched his steward swirl her around. Aonghus murmured something in Lila's ear which made her toss her head back and laugh. Jealousy pierced him; he told himself that Aonghus knew he and Lila had been lovers, and he would never cross such a line with her. Yet this knowledge didn't stop the acrid taste of bitterness in his mouth.

"Do ye like my gown, my laird?" Achdara asked, trying to draw his attention back to her. "Ye used tae like this one verrae much."

He reluctantly tore his gaze away from Lila to focus on Achdara, glancing with disinterest at the gown she wore. It was a forest-green gown with a low-cut bodice that she'd kept trying to draw his attention to. When he'd considered courting her, he had liked the gown on her, but he now realized that the mild interest he'd once felt toward her was but a trace of the fiery desire he felt toward Lila. As he studied Achdara, he now wondered how he'd found her cold, austere looks pleasing to the eye. Lila was warmth, joy, and laughter, a burst of light that had rid him of the shadows of his grief. And God, how he missed her.

Achdara must have taken note of the disinterest in his eyes, because her expression hardened, her gaze sweeping to Lila. There was no mistaking the jealousy that tightened her features.

"Is she yer mistress now, my laird?" she asked coolly. "I should have kent the Sassenach would behave like a common whore. With the way she's dancing with Aonghus—"

"Ye'll not speak of her that way." The growl that tore from his throat made Achdara go pale, and she swallowed. "She's my guest. I'll have ye removed from my side if ye continue tae insult her, Lady McNabb."

His use of her married name was purposeful. Hurt flickered in her eyes and she lowered her head.

"I will take my leave, my laird. I didnae intend tae cause ye any offence."

She reached out to place her hand on his arm, and he looked down at it with irritation. A mere touch of Lila's hand on his flesh filled him with heat, Achdara's left him cold. She dropped her hand.

"I bid ye good night, my laird."

As Achdara walked away, he turned his focus back to Lila. She and Aonghus had finished their dance, and she was now looking right at him, a hardness in her lovely eyes as Aonghus escorted her back to her seat; she must have seen Achdara touch him. A part of him was delighted at her obvious jealousy, though he tried to communicate with his eyes that Achdara meant nothing to him, that her touch left him cold, but Lila had already averted her gaze.

Aonghus took Achdara's vacant seat, giving him a teasing grin.

"Ye looked like ye wanted tae murder me just now," he said cheerfully. "I've never seen ye so jealous over a lass. 'Tis quite amusing."

A denial sprang to his lips about being jealous, but he couldn't speak the lie. He'd felt possessive over Lila even before he'd taken her innocence, and despite his knowledge of what she was and where—when—she was truly from, he couldn't help but consider her his.

"Then ye'll take care nae tae dance with her going forward," he said, his scowl deepening, but this seemed to only amuse Aonghus more.

"I ken ye care for the lass," Aonghus said, as Lila stood to leave the hall. He wanted to follow but watched her go, with a pang.

"It doesnae matter," Gawen said, tearing his gaze away from her retreating form. "She has her duty, and I have mine."

"Gawen." Aonghus's tone turned serious. "Ye've done nothing but focus on yer duties as laird since yer family died. 'Tis nae a sin tae enjoy some happiness, however brief it may be."

Aonghus gave him a long look before another noble pulled him into conversation, and Gawen mulled over his words. He'd focused on his duties to keep from drowning in his grief. But since Lila's arrival, his grief had dissipated. It was still there, as he suspected it would always be, but it wasn't as stark as it had once been.

When Gawen headed to his chamber later, he made a decision. Aonghus was right; he wanted to bask in the light of Lila's presence for as long as she was here. Gawen wanted a bit of happiness before he returned to a life of duty; they would just have to not lose focus of tracking down Malmuira.

Now he just had to get his Lila to open up to him again. A lightness filled him at the thought as he entered his chamber. He would see her on the morrow after tending to his duties and ask if she wanted to go for a ride.

Smiling at the thought, he froze at the sight that greeted him when he entered his chamber.

Achdara sat on the edge of his bed, clad in a loose underdress that she'd lowered to reveal her breasts, her golden hair flowing freely around her shoulders. Fury filled him, and he opened his mouth to demand that she leave at once, when he heard a sharp gasp behind him.

He whirled. Lila stood in his doorway, her face drained of color, the devastation plain on her features as she took in Achdara.

"Lila—" he began, but she'd already fled from his chamber. The look of triumph on Achdara's face made his fury burn even brighter.

"Get out," he hissed. "Ye are tae leave the castle at once. I'll have my guard escort ye tae yer manor."

"Gawen—" Achdara protested, her triumph vanishing.

"Get out of my castle," he repeated, turning on his feet to follow the only woman he cared for. The only woman he needed.

CHAPTER 20

Hot tears stung Lila's eyes as she stumbled back to her chamber. The sight of Gawen with Achdara had torn her heart in two. She kept telling herself that it was none of her business, that the night they'd shared would be the only thing that ever happened between them and she had no claim over him, yet that didn't stop the jealousy, the heartache.

She'd gone to his chamber under the pretense of asking him if they could question Kudan to uncover what he was hiding. In reality, she'd just wanted an excuse to be alone with him; she missed him more than she should. But the sight of him with Achdara . . .

"Lila."

She stiffened at the sound of his voice behind her and whirled, anger and jealousy gnawing at her belly.

"I didn't mean to interrupt you and your mistress," she said tightly. "I apologize for—"

She stopped with a gasp as he crossed the chamber in several long strides, reaching out to gently grip her by the arms.

"Achdara snuck intae my chamber. I didnae ken she was there. I just sent her away from the castle. I donnae want Achdara. All I've been able tae think about is ye. *Only* ye. I'd just decided that I missed ye—needed ye—tae much tae stay away. Do ye ken how jealous I was watching ye dance with Aonghus? How I wanted tae tear him apart with my bare hands—a man who's like a brother tae me? Achdara, nor any lass, has ever caused me such jealousy. I only want ye, Lila," he rasped. "And damn me, I ken what we agreed. But I cannae stay away."

He crashed his mouth to hers in a hungry kiss. She stiffened in momentary surprise, her anger and jealousy replaced by the ever-present ache she felt for Gawen, that invisible thread of desire that bound her to him. That love. Her heart thundered against her chest as she returned his kiss, breathing in the masculine scent of him, winding her hands through his silken, red strands, her body coming alive as if it had been asleep during the time they'd kept their distance from each other.

He wrapped his arms around her waist, binding her to him in a viselike grip as if he feared she'd try to break free, but she leaned in even closer to him. God, she needed him. She loved him. All thoughts of Achdara and Malmuira had vanished; there was only Gawen, this man from another time who'd stolen her heart.

Gawen let out a low groan as he walked with her until her back was against the wall. She melted against him as he hiked up her skirts with one hand. His finger dipped into her flooded center, and she gasped against his mouth, a torrent of pleasure rushing through her body as he stroked her.

She whimpered as he continued to stroke, his mouth never leaving hers as tendrils of pleasure tightened their hold on her body. She could feel the beginnings of her climax, and Gawen didn't stop stroking her or dominating her mouth even as her climax tore through her and she let out a cry, her body quaking against him.

Only then did he tear his mouth from hers, keeping her in the circle of his arms as she floated down from the high of her orgasm.

"Ye look like a siren, my Lila," he rasped, his eyes raking her in from head to toe, as she struggled to catch her breath. "'Tis been torture tae keep my distance from ye, after I've already taken ye're innocence. Ye're mine, sweet Lila. All mine." His voice deepened to a possessive growl, and Lila shuddered with pleasure at the raw need in his eyes.

He claimed her mouth in another kiss, this one a branding, a claiming. *He doesn't need to claim me,* Lila thought, through the haze of her pleasure. *I'm already his. Every part of me.*

"I cannae wait," he continued, his words a desperate rasp against her mouth. "I must have ye now..."

"Gawen," she cried out on a moan, as he released himself from his kilt and buried his cock inside her, reaching out to anchor her to him by her hips as he thrust, all the while keeping his mouth molded against hers. She held tightly to him as they moved together, their breaths coming out in sharp gasps as he pounded her against the wall.

It wasn't long before Lila could feel the rise of another climax, that stirring of pleasure that began in her center and expanded, and she cried out as her second orgasm tore through her. Gawen's release came soon after; he let out a deep growl as he spilled himself inside her.

If Gawen hadn't held her up, Lila would have melted onto the floor. He reached out to swing her up into his arms, bridal style, his green eyes mischievous as he carried her to the bed, where he divested her of her gown, seizing one of her nipples in his mouth. Lila threw her head back, letting out a whimper of pleasure.

"That was only the beginning, sweet Lila," he murmured, releasing her breast from his mouth as he peppered kisses down her abdomen. "I intend tae have ye again ... and again ..."

Lila had to clamp her hand over her mouth to stifle her scream as Gawen once again brought her to the heights of pleasure.

~

"I MISSED YE SO, SWEET LILA," he whispered afterward, burying his face in her hair. "And nae just yer presence in my bed. I care about ye, lass. Ye've brought joy tae my life again. It was folly tae think we should keep our distance. We can keep focus better if we're together. While ye're here, we should enjoy each other."

Lila's heart had begun to swell until he said the words "while ye're here." Her chest constricted, and she swallowed a lump in her throat.

He's right, she told herself. He didn't know the depths of her feelings for him, and nothing had inherently changed; she was still a time-traveling witch, and he was still a fourteenth-century Scottish laird who'd need to marry a suitable bride. She had her life in the future: her family, her coven. But this didn't fill her with joy; instead, a sharp pain pierced her at the thought of a life without Gawen.

"Why did ye come tae my chamber?" Gawen asked now, sitting up and pinning her with curious green eyes.

"I wanted to suggest we go talk to Kudan again," she said, burying her anguish as she forced a smile. "And then I saw Achdara..."

"She shouldnae have gotten in. I'm going tae have a word with my guard. I can only glean she kens I desire ye, and she thought tae offer me her body," Gawen said with a scowl.

"You weren't interested at all?" Lila asked, her lingering jealousy once again rising to the surface. "Inghean told me you're going to possibly marry her."

Gawen let out an annoyed grunt. "I told ye Inghean rarely speaks truth. I donnae want

Achdara. I've nae been able tae even think of another lass since meeting ye."

Warmth returned to Lila's body, chasing away her jealousy, and she tugged him down for a deep kiss. When they broke apart for air, he reached out to stroke her hair.

"'Tis a fine idea tae talk tae Kudan again," he said. "On the way back from his home, if the weather is fair, we should enjoy another . . ." He paused, searching for the word, his handsome features creased in concentration. "Picniba."

"Picnic," Lila corrected, grinning.

"There are many strange words from yer time," Gawen said with a playful scowl. He turned a bashful gaze at her, tracing her face with his fingertips. "Would ye like tae enjoy a picnic on the morrow?"

"You already have me in bed, and you're shy about asking me out on a date?" Lila teased.

"Date?" Gawen asked. "A date on the calendar? Or is this another odd word from yer time?"

"In my time, it also means . . . to woo. What people do when they're considering a relationship or marriage."

She froze at her words, concerned that Gawen would misunderstand. But he didn't look uneasy.

"Ye donnae need tae worry," he said, taking in her embarrassed flush. "I ken we cannae marry," he added lightly, his calm words causing shards of pain to pierce her heart. "But I would like tae woo ye, while ye're here."

"I'd like that," she said, forcing a smile, hoping that he couldn't detect her heartbreak.

As Gawen drifted off to sleep moments later, keeping her enfolded in his arms, she reached out to brush back a stray lock of hair from his handsome face. The firelight danced off his angular features, illuminating every detail—that strong jaw, the sensual mouth that had given her such pleasure. He had ruined her for every other man. No one would be able to compare to Gawen, the man she'd fallen in love with in the past.

If circumstances were different, what kind of future would they have together? Once again, she allowed herself to fantasize about this possible future—sitting at Gawen's side during feasts, practicing her spells in the lush groves that dotted the island, spending their nights together in his bed. And that persistent, aching thought of children, a brood of boys and girls with Gawen's fiery, red hair.

Her parents and sister were time travelers, she wouldn't be giving up a life with them if she stayed in this time; they could visit. Gawen's handsomeness would certainly impress her sister; she could imagine the mischievous wink Avery would give her at the sight of Gawen, something she did any time a handsome man crossed their path. His honor and commitment to duty would impress her protective parents.

The longing that consumed her at the thought of her family meeting Gawen, of their potential children, caused a wave of pure joy to sweep over her. She did want that future, badly, but it would not be.

Gawen had just told her they couldn't marry; he'd made it clear to her when they first met that he intended to marry a suitable Scottish bride.

Lila closed her eyes, blinking back the sudden sting of tears; she'd been overemotional lately. She had to force her thoughts away from her longing, focusing instead on the dark, evasive Malmuira—and Kudan. She had the feeling she was missing something crucial, but she couldn't fathom what it was. Why had Malmuira spared Kudan? If Kudan's descendant caused this massacre and she wanted to stop it, the simplest way would have been to kill Kudan.

She expelled a sigh and started to lift her hand from her belly, where it had unconsciously drifted when she'd fantasized about having Gawen's children.

But she froze, her heart picking up its pace, her hand still resting on her flat belly. She recalled the look on Ysenda's face as she'd looked at Kudan. It had been a fleeting look, lasting for no longer than a second, but now Lila recognized it. It was a look of longing. Of love. The same longing Lila had for Gawen. Ysenda had barely looked at her own husband, Struan.

Ysenda and Kudan are having an affair. She sat up in bed so abruptly that Gawen stirred beside her. That was what Kudan was hiding—it had to be.

But she suspected their affair was just the cusp of what Kudan was hiding. She now realized what she'd been missing, what had been staring her in the face all along. She wanted to curse herself for not seeing it before.

"What is it?" Gawen asked, sitting up with a worried frown. "Lila?"

"We've been focusing on the wrong person," Lila said, panic coursing through her veins like wildfire. "I know who Malmuira's real target is."

CHAPTER 21

Gawen kicked the sides of his horse, racing ahead of Lila, Aonghus, and his guards. His heart pounded in his chest, Lila's revelation still echoing in his mind.

"I believe Ysenda and Kudan are having an affair. I think Ysenda is pregnant, and the man who causes the massacre is her descendant. Malmuira must have realized this, and that's why she didn't kill Kudan—Ysenda is the true target."

After her momentous words, he and Lila had dressed and raced out of her chamber. If they could have, Lila would have used a Transport spell, but such a spell wouldn't be able to transport the guards he wanted to take with them as a precaution, and they couldn't risk being seen by someone who didn't know about the stiuireadh. Instead, they'd taken the fastest two horses in the stables after he'd gathered several guards to accompany them to Struan and Ysenda's home. Gawen knew he'd have to deal with Struan, who wouldn't react well to the knowledge that his wife not only was having an affair with his cousin but was pregnant by him. The important thing was keeping Ysenda safe and preventing Malmuira from murdering her and her unborn child.

His body went cold with dread at the thought of the future massacre Malmuira was trying to prevent. He could understand wanting to prevent such a tragedy; he knew the pain of loss well, and he could only imagine her anguish and fury. He'd wanted the stiuireadh to prevent the deaths of his family using their ability. But the comparison ended there; he'd never murder others to prevent his own loss, and certainly not a lass who carried an innocent bairn.

His determination increased, and he leaned forward on his horse as he picked up speed.

When they arrived at Struan and Ysenda's home, a large cottage not far from the village, he had his men surround it to make certain it was secure. A surprised looking servant answered the door; Gawen and Lila moved past her without a word and entered the main room, where Ysenda stood up in surprise, lowering her embroidery.

"Laird MacRaild—" she began, startled.

"Where is yer husband?" Gawen asked tersely.

"He's gone tae the village. Why? Has something happened?"

Relief skittered through him. It was best that Struan wasn't here for this confrontation. He looked at Lila and gave her a nod; they'd decided it was best if she asked Ysenda the delicate questions.

Lila stepped forward, taking Ysenda's hands. Ysenda stiffened, regarding her with wariness.

"I'm going to ask you a question," Lila said gently. "It's very important that you tell me the truth."

Ysenda hesitated, but she gave Lila a shaky nod.

"Are you with child?" Lila asked.

Ysenda froze, the color draining from her face.

"How—how did ye ken?" she asked.

Gawen's heart plummeted in his chest at her confession; a part of him had hoped that Lila was wrong. He wasn't looking forward to dealing with her husband's anger, and the revenge he'd want to enact on Kudan.

"It doesn't matter right now," Lila said, giving her a smile that was kind and without judgment. "All that matters is keeping you and your baby safe."

"Why? Why would I nae be safe?"

"I'll tell you, but it's important that you answer this next question honestly as well," Lila said. "Who is the father of your baby?"

Ysenda swallowed hard, her gaze straying to Gawen.

"Why, my husband, of—of course," she said shakily. Gawen could tell it was a lie, a married woman accused of her husband not being the father of her unborn bairn would have shown more outrage. "I donnae ken what ye've heard, but—"

"Ysenda, there's no time for this," Gawen barked, ignoring Lila's sharp look as he stepped forward. He knew they needed to tread delicately with Ysenda, but there was too much at stake. "Tell us the truth. Who is the father of yer bairn? No punishment will come tae ye; I'll handle yer husband. But ye must tell us the truth."

Ysenda's face crumpled; she sank down onto her chair.

"The bairn—'tis Kudan's," she whispered. "But I love him, and he loves me. We—we were planning tae leave Skye, tae start a new life in the Highlands. Kudan has coin he inherited from his father. He was going tae tell Struan, but I wanted to wait, because I was afeared of—"

"'Tis all right," Gawen interrupted, his heart hammering. "Ye and yer bairn are in danger. I'm taking ye tae the castle where ye'll be put under guard."

Ysenda gasped, her hands flying to her mouth.

"I—I ken Struan will be upset, but he's nae a violent man, I donnae think he will harm me."

"It's not Struan we're concerned with," Lila said gently. "We'll tell you everything, but we need to get you out of here. You should pack whatever you need."

Ysenda looked hesitant, but at Gawen's hard look, she scrambled out of the room, calling for her servant to help her pack.

Once she left, Lila raised a shaking hand to her temple, and Gawen realized that her calm manner with Ysenda had been for appearances' sake; she now looked terrified.

"I'll have to put a Cloaking spell on her before

she leaves to go to the castle. If Malmuira comes searching for her there, she'll kill anyone in her path to get to her. She needs to think Ysenda is still here, and"—Lila licked her lips, her skin growing paler as she continued—"I need to be here to confront her when she does."

Panic flooded Gawen's body. He stepped forward to grasp her arms, shaking his head.

"No," he rasped, "Lila, ye cannae—"

"This is what I came here to do," Lila interrupted. "I need to be the one to stop her. I don't know if Malmuira has figured out Ysenda is her true target yet, but there's no time to waste."

The look Lila leveled him with was firm; he knew there would be no swaying her. Fear like he'd never known before swept over him. What if Malmuira killed her?

Lila seemed to read his thoughts, reaching up to touch the sides of his face and giving him a reassuring smile.

"Leave guards here if you must, but this is what I was sent here to do," she whispered.

Gawen gave her a grudging nod, still consumed with anxiety and fear. He had his men take Ysenda to his horse after Lila performed a Cloaking spell on her; Ysenda looked both confused and horrified as Lila performed the spells. He had much to explain to Ysenda once they reached the castle.

Gawen ordered two of his men to stay behind, but he would send at least one more. Given the men he had patrolling the lands and the castle, he couldn't spare more, though he would have sent them all to protect Lila if he could. He vowed that he would return tonight after tending to his duties. He wanted to spend as much time as he could at her side, keeping her safe.

Before he left, he enfolded Lila in his arms, giving her a searing kiss, not caring that they were in full view of his guards. There was an ocean of things he wanted to say: how much he cared for her, how he feared for her, how he didn't want to leave her side, not for a moment. His throat tightened as he gazed down at her, pressing his forehead to hers.

"Be safe, my Lila," he whispered, the only words he could conjure, before he turned and forced himself to leave her behind.

CHAPTER 22

After Gawen left with Ysenda and his men, leaving two behind to stand guard outside of Struan's home, Lila moved from room to room, using Olfactory spells to enhance Ysenda's natural scent from the belongings she'd left behind. She needed Malmuira to think Ysenda was still here.

When she'd infused every room in the house—even the outdoor garden in the back—with Ysenda's scent, she buried herself in the Arsa grimoire, which she'd grabbed in haste before leaving the castle, reviewing every Offensive and Defensive spell she could find, committing them to memory.

As she reviewed the spells, queasiness rose in her stomach, queasiness she attributed to nerves. That familiar uncertainty tried to take hold of her, to tell her she wasn't strong enough, that Malmuira would kill not only her but Gawen and anyone who stood in her way. She forced herself to quell her fears, making herself eat a meal of vegetable stew that Ysenda's servant had been preparing before they sent her away for her safety.

Struan arrived just after midday; she could hear him arguing with the guards outside until they directed him to the castle. Lila's stomach tightened; she hoped Gawen was prepared to deal with a raging, jealous husband. Infidelity wasn't taken lightly in her own time; she had no doubt that Struan would want to murder Kudan once he learned the truth.

After she resumed reviewing more Offensive and Defensive spells she could use in her battle against Malmuira, her nausea rose; she had to go to the privy to vomit. She leaned back against the wall after emptying the contents of her stomach, praying her anxiety would settle; she needed to be at her best when Malmuira appeared.

To her surprise, Gawen arrived with a small sack swung over his shoulder as the sky grew dark, and she was preparing herself a dinner of leftover vegetable stew. Delight coursed through her at the sight of him, though it dissipated as he approached her with a frown.

"Are ye unwell? Ye look pale."

"I'm just nervous about facing Malmuira."

His frown deepened. He cupped her face, his gaze raking over her with concern.

"If ye're nae well—"

"I am well," she interjected, her tone coming out sharper than she intended, but she knew where this was going. "I'm ready to fight her and end this. How is Ysenda? Did Struan show up?"

He scowled, seeming to realize she was changing the subject, but he answered her question without pressing the matter.

"She's fine, under guard by my best men. Kudan is there; he insisted on staying at her side. Struan arrived, aye; me and Aonghus had tae restrain him from attacking Kudan. He's more humiliated than jealous or even angered—it proves he never truly loved the lass. He agreed tae a divorce; I gave him a settlement of land. I ordered Kudan and Struan tae never see each other again. Struan has vowed to put him tae his blade if they ever cross paths. 'Tis good that Ysenda and Kudan plan tae relocate tae the Highlands when this matter with Malmuira is handled." He dropped his hands from her face, offering her one of his devastating smiles. "I'll stay with ye for the night and return tae the castle in the morning."

"No, Gawen. It's too dangerous. Malmuira will kill you," she said, though her stomach fluttered with joy at the thought of spending the night with him.

"I'm nae leaving ye," he growled. "During the day, aye, I must be at the castle tae tend tae my duties, but I will be returning here. I may nae have magic, but I'll do what I can tae protect ye."

There was a fierce, primal protectiveness in his expression, one that caused warmth to spiral through her belly, even as her worry increased. As strong of a warrior Gawen no doubt was, he was no match against magic.

"Fine," she said grudgingly, knowing there was

nothing she could say to make him return to the castle. "But you must do as I say if and when she arrives. I'll put a Binding spell on you if I have to."

Gawen's scowl dissipated; he gave her a smile that was both rakish and mischievous.

"I can think of another reason ye can put a Binding spell on me," he murmured, and a blazing heat infused her at the images his words evoked.

His expression shifted, and he looked a little shy as he gestured to the sack on his shoulder.

"I also came here for us tae have a night . . . picnic," he said, taking great effort to pronounce the word "picnic" correctly, which was so adorable that she had to smile. "I ken we had tae take care of Ysenda and Kudan, but that doesnae mean we cannae have a moment of peace tae dine."

Lila beamed, the tension in her shoulders ebbing. She'd done all the spells she could for the day, and there were men standing guard at the door. It wouldn't hurt to share a romantic night picnic with the man she loved.

"I'd like that," Lila said, and Gawen grinned, gesturing for her to follow as they made their way out to the back garden.

They enjoyed a meal of freshly baked bread and succulent roasted pork marinated in honey that the castle's cook had prepared, eating the savory meal with their hands. Lila was glad that her queasiness had subsided, at least for the moment, and she inhaled the damp night air as they ate in companionable silence.

"It's difficult to see the night sky so clearly in my

time," she said, looking up at the multitude of stars that blanketed the sky. "I only see skies like this when my family takes camping trips out to the mountains."

"Ye cannae see the night sky?"

"City lights and pollution clog up the sky, especially near large cities. There's nothing like the night sky in the Highlands. Especially in this time," she said with a wistful sigh.

"Aye," he agreed, following her gaze up to the sky. "Sometimes when I went hunting with Father, we'd make camp overnight in groves. Nights like these were perfect when it wasnae tae hot or cold. That's when he would tell me tales of his father, of growing up at Carraig Castle, of the Norsemen our ancestors fought."

A look of nostalgia flickered across his face. Lila leaned back and watched him, enjoying the soothing timbre of his voice as he told her how his sister would sometimes join them, even though he used to resent her presence because he wanted the alone time with his father.

"But now I appreciate those moments we had together," he said, a small smile tugging at his lips.

She reached out and linked her hand through his, and he pulled her close, burying his head in her hair.

"I missed ye today," he confessed, and her heart swelled. He reached down to tilt her head up so that their eyes locked. "Have ye bewitched me, sweet Lila?"

"Perhaps," she teased, running her hand across

the broad expanse of his chest, taking pleasure in the way his breath hitched at her touch.

"Since ye've arrived in this time, I've nae been able tae focus," he murmured, reaching out to pull her onto his lap, and she gasped at the feel of his arousal. "I feel as if ye're a ray of sunlight that's entered my life, chasing away the shadows."

"Oh, Gawen," she murmured, his words moving her. They weren't a confession of love, but they were close; she suddenly realized how much she ached for him to say the words. *I love ye, Lila.* It was on the tip of her tongue to confess her love for him, but when he leaned in to kiss her, she forgot her own name. His kiss was firm and demanding, sending spirals of heat coiling around her body. He released her mouth and peppered kisses down the side of her jaw, her throat, lower . . .

"Gawen," she gasped, taking in their surroundings. "We're outside."

"Are we?" he teased with a wicked grin. "We're in a private back garden. I have a second cloak tae put over us. And the guards won't disturb us. I ordered them nae tae interrupt unless there was any sign of danger."

Lila needed no further convincing. She arched back as Gawen kissed the flesh above her bodice, lowering it to seize a nipple with his mouth, teasing it with his tongue. She gasped, pressing her hand to her mouth to stifle her cry as he laved her nipple, before turning his focus to her other breast.

She was breathless with pleasure when he lowered her to the cloak on the ground before covering them both with a second cloak, shielding their bodies from view as he again seized her lips with his, reaching down to stroke her moist center.

"Gawen," she whispered, arching her body toward him as his ministrations made her body come to life.

"Come for me, sweet Lila," he whispered against her mouth, and she obliged, her body coming apart as her climax rippled through her.

"Ye're so verrae lovely," he whispered, releasing himself from his kilt, and she reached down to stroke the long hardness of his cock, making him hiss with pleasure. "I must have ye."

He sank inside her, reaching up to grasp her wrists, and Lila let out a soft moan at the sweet feel of him moving inside her. The grass beneath the cloak rubbed against her back as Gawen speared her center with powerful thrusts, keeping her body wedged to his as he kissed her, his body imitating the movements of his lips. The cool night air permeated the cloak, chilling their heated skin as they moved together, until the pleasure that flared to life in her belly once more grew, and Gawen swallowed up her cry as they found their release together.

Afterward, he stood up and hefted her into his arms as if she weighed nothing, taking her inside to the spare room. There, he tucked her close into his side, fusing his mouth to hers, and they made love once more before drifting off to a peaceful sleep in each other's arms.

When she awoke, a stab of disappointment pierced her to find Gawen gone, even though she knew he'd return to the castle in the morning.

She began her usual ritual of practicing her spells after the guards informed her they'd seen nothing out of the ordinary last night. Unease crawled through her at this; she prayed Malmuira hadn't determined Ysenda was at the castle and intended to strike there.

She was making herself a warm vegetable broth using leftover scraps in the kitchen to quell her queasy stomach when Coira arrived. Lila took her in with surprise, stepping forward to embrace her.

"Coira! What are you doing here?"

"The laird told me ye were here awaiting this dark witch—Malmuira. I thought I could help ye," Coira said.

"But . . . you said you barely have any power."

"Barely, aye," Coira said with a smile edged with danger. "But that doesnae mean I have none."

With a mischievous grin, she gestured for Lila to follow her to the kitchen.

"Witchcraft is more than just the conjuring of spells," Coira said, gesturing to a small sack of herbs she'd brought with her. "There's a craft tae it, creating drafts and concoctions that can make spells more potent, or work their own magic."

Lila watched, transfixed, as Coira made one particular concoction using herbs she'd grown in her garden along with a fragrant wine that she'd enchanted; the combination of the two could enhance a Transformational spell. Lila smiled, impressed by her knowledge. Coira may not think she had much power, but she knew more about the craft of magic than any other witch she'd encountered.

As Coira explained the order of ingredients for a particular draft that could aid a Sleep spell, Lila couldn't quell her rising nausea. She raced out of the kitchen to the privy, where she again emptied the contents of her stomach.

When she came out, Coira was already waiting for her with a mug of hot broth and a knowing smile.

"I couldnae keep anything down when I was pregnant with my first bairn," she said matter-of-factly.

Lila froze, almost spilling the mug of broth.

"Pregnant?"

"Aye," Coira returned, her smile widening. "I could tell as soon as I saw ye; I can always tell. 'Tis early days yet, but ye're carrying a wee bairn. And if I may hazard a guess, I'd say it belongs tae the handsome laird."

Lila leaned back against the wall, shaking. She'd been so consumed in practicing spells, obsessing over Malmuira's location and her growing love for Gawen that she'd not even considered that she could be pregnant. She'd assumed her heightened emotions and queasiness were all on account of nerves. If she was pregnant, she must have conceived the first night she'd spent with Gawen.

They hadn't used anything, and she hadn't taken the birth control pill she took to regulate her periods since arriving in this time. Then again, she certainly hadn't expected to make love to anyone here.

But as her shock—and annoyance at herself, for not even considering pregnancy—rose, so did a wave of pure joy. Her hand drifted to her stomach. Would her child be a boy, with Gawen's red hair and sparkling green eyes? Or a girl, with her brunette hair and blue eyes? She allowed herself to bask in her joy for only a moment before reality settled in.

Gawen. She had to tell Gawen. She knew that pregnant women could travel through time, though it could be risky. But her heart clenched at the thought of leaving Gawen. Did she even want to return to her own time?

"Ye're thinking tae much, dear," Coira said, taking her arm and guiding her back to the kitchen. "I'll concoct a draft that will confirm if ye're pregnant or nae, but I'm rarely wrong about these things."

Lila sat tensely as Coira prepared a draft, handing it to her with a kind smile. After Lila drank the concoction, which had a bittersweet flavor, Coira placed her hand on Lila's, and they both placed her hands on her flat belly.

"This spell is an old one, passed down by druid midwives. The spell willnae harm the bairn," Coira said. "Repeat after me. *Nochdadh lathaireachd mo bairn dhomh.*"

Lila repeated the words of the spell with Coira,

and a rush of warmth spread over her. She froze as she could feel the faint, steady hum of *life* beneath her hands, along with a swell of overwhelming love.

There was indeed a baby growing in her belly. Her child. Her and Gawen's child.

CHAPTER 23

As Lila lay in bed that night, her hand resting on her flat belly, a rush of emotions washing over her. After Coira had retired to the spare room for the night, one of the guards told Lila that Gawen wouldn't be coming that night as he had an urgent matter to tend to at the castle. Though she'd felt a stab of disappointment, a part of her was relieved. She didn't know if she was prepared for Gawen's reaction. She wasn't the suitable Scottish bride he'd mentioned weeks earlier, and she was a stiuireadh, a person he inherently distrusted.

She knew that he wouldn't want her to fight Malmuira, something that Lila had only briefly considered—briefly. Witches could perform powerful spells even in late pregnancy. *Magic is what our bodies were meant for, no matter the state*, her mother had once told her. She was even more determined to defeat Malmuira now, knowing that her target was another pregnant woman. She wouldn't let anything happen to Ysenda's unborn child, no matter what the future held.

She drifted off to sleep with her hand still pressed to her belly. But unlike the blissful sleep she'd had in Gawen's arms the night before, dark dreams punctuated her slumber, just like the ones she'd had before arriving in this time, and the ones she'd had back at the inn.

Lila awoke from one particular nightmare in which she was drowning, with a multitude of white fingers pushing her head beneath dark, murky waters. No matter how hard she struggled she couldn't resurface, water entering her lungs as she fought to breathe.

She sat up with a gasp, trembling violently, and froze when she realized there was another presence in the room. She frowned in confusion; it was Mysie. She stood standing at the foot of her bed, looking at her with a blank expression.

"Mysie?" she asked. "What are you—"

She fell into a horrified silence as Mysie's form shifted before her eyes; the plain, mousy girl transforming to a gray-eyed, dark-haired woman who glowered at her. Icy fear curled around Lila's body, along with disbelief. It was the woman she'd seen in her dream when she'd glimpsed the dark witch—the woman Kudan had described.

This was Malmuira.

Malmuira gave her a smile that chilled Lila to the bone, raising her hands. Panic tore through Lila as Malmuira shouted a spell into the darkness, one she didn't recognize. Lila retaliated by shouting an

Offensive spell, darting out of bed to evade Malmuira's spell.

Malmuira let out a hiss of frustration, casting a Binding spell before Lila could evade or counter. The spell hurled Lila against the wall and pinned her immobile, powerless. Malmuira advanced, hot fury shooting from her eyes.

"Why are ye here in this time?" she spat. "I didnae kill ye before because I donnae want tae harm one of my kind. I thought ye were harmless at first, one of those witches who traveled through time out of curiosity. But ye're nae here for that, are ye?"

"I'm here to stop you!" Lila shouted. "I know what you're doing. I know about the massacre—the massacre that takes place two centuries from now that you're trying to prevent."

Malmuira stilled with surprise, and Lila saw a brief flicker of grief in the depths of her gray eyes before rage replaced it.

"It doesnae concern ye!" she roared. "I donnae want tae kill my own kind, but I will if I must."

"Who was it?" Lila demanded, desperate to buy time to recall the counter to the Binding spell that held her immobile. "Who did you lose in the massacre?"

Malmuira's face blanched, and there was that grief again, contorting her features into a mask of anguish.

"'Tis not who I lost—'tis what I lost. I lost everything," Malmuira rasped, tears shining in her eyes. Lila now saw why her nightmares of Malmuira were infused with such rage, such grief. Both emotions burned bright from Malmuira, as bright as the heat from a raging fire. "I lost everything in that massacre, and I'm going tae get it back! I willnae let ye stop me."

She raised her hand to issue a spell, but Lila had recalled the counter to the Binding spell just in time, releasing herself from its paralyzing hold.

Frustration filled Malmuira's features, and she advanced, opening her mouth to shout another spell. But Lila was faster.

"*Tha mi a 'guidhe or gundean thu an t'aingidha seo bleed!*" Lila cried.

Malmuira stumbled to her knees, her eyes widening in horrified surprise as she clutched the wound that had appeared on the side of her neck, the wound caused by Lila's spell. It wasn't fatal, but it would incapacitate her.

Lila ventured forward, murmuring a Binding spell to hold Malmuira still.

"I was sent here to stop you—to kill you. But even after what you've done, I believe in mercy. If you allow me to transport you back to your time, to keep you there, you will only have to face your coven for what you've done."

"What I've done?" Malmuira bellowed, her eyes narrowing.

"Those innocent farmers you killed—Clinnen and Daimh. Attacking Kudan. And Mysie? I take it you killed her for the Transformational spell? It's how you glamoured yourself to look like her, isn't it?"

Lila now recalled with a chill the long, probing look "Mysie" had given her when she'd fished for gossip back at the castle. She thought she'd just unnerved her by her questions. Little did she know that sweet, shy Mysie was likely dead at that point, and Malmuira had taken her place.

And she recalled the sensation of someone watching her in the corridor outside of the great hall . . . that must have also been Malmuira.

The defiant glare Malmuira gave her confirmed her suspicions, and Lila's fury rose.

"I was mistaken about those farmers, aye, and Kudan Munroe. My spells werenae precise; I thought they were the ones who needed tae die, but I was wrong. I didnae even want tae travel this far back, just back far enough tae stop the massacre, tae warn those who were killed. But this is the only time I could travel back tae," Malmuira spat, though there was a brief flicker of shame in her eyes.

"And what about Sgaire? The man from Clan MacRaild, who's helping you?" Lila asked, ice filling her veins. "Did you kill him too?"

"He served his purpose and guided me here from Tairseach. He was a traitorous rat, willing tae turn on his clan for sweet words and a night in my bed. I did a service tae his clan by ending his life," Malmuira said, and this time there was no regret in her stormy eyes.

"Don't you see what you're doing? By trying to prevent what will happen, you're causing more pain and destruction, *more* death. You have to stop!" Lila cried. "Don't make me have to kill you!"

Although there were tears in her eyes, Malmuira gave her a look of angry defiance. Lila felt another stab of pity for Malmuira; she had allowed her grief and rage to consume her.

"I'll never stop," Malmuira vowed. "Never. I will prevent that massacre. I must!"

Lila closed her eyes, expelling a breath. She'd tried to offer her mercy. Now she would do what she must.

Her hands trembling, she raised them to issue the Killing spell, but before she could open her mouth, Malmuira vanished before her eyes.

Panic tore through Lila, she stared at the spot Malmuira had just occupied in horror as the door flew open and Coira rushed in.

"I heard her in here—I tried tae get in, but she did something tae the door. I couldnae enter," Coira said, hurrying forward and helping Lila to her feet. "Did she harm ye?"

"No," Lila replied, frustration swelling. Because of her, Malmuira had escaped. "I injured her and gave her a chance to stop. When she refused, I was on the verge of killing her, but she vanished. I shouldn't have shown her mercy."

"Mercy is the way of the stiuireadh," Coira said, giving her hands a reassuring squeeze. "You did what any good witch would do."

Lila removed her hands from Coira's and moved toward the door; now was not the time for regret and reassurances. Panic constricted her throat, making it hard to breathe. Gawen was at the castle. If Malmuira harmed him . . .

"We need to get to the castle—now," Lila said, her voice quavering with fear. "Malmuira knows Ysenda isn't here."

Coira nodded her agreement, and together they hurried out of the house, freezing at the sight that greeted them when they arrived outside.

The three guards all lay dead.

Fury and nausea washed over Lila at the sight, and she swayed on her feet. She had been a fool to show Malmuira mercy.

"There was nothing ye could have done," Coira said, taking in the look of guilt on her face.

But the guilt remained as Coira took both of her hands in her own, murmuring the words of the Transport spell that took them to Carraig Castle.

~

"Lila!"

Gawen rushed into the great hall where the guards had ushered both her and Coira, his face pale with both terror and relief as he strode toward her, enfolding her in his arms. She clung to him, her heart pounding in tandem with his, before he pulled back.

"Did Malmuira harm ye?"

"No. I injured her before she vanished. Gawen, she glamoured herself to look like Mysie, my personal maid. She was under my nose the whole time."

Anger at herself rose within her gut, and she swallowed hard. How could she not have known?

Gawen gave her shoulders a comforting squeeze, even as his features went even more pale.

"Ye couldnae have kent; she fooled us all. But Mysie has been at my castle for years; I thought Malmuira only arrived recently."

"She did—she killed the real Mysie and used a Transformational spell to take on her likeness," Lila whispered, a chill spreading throughout her body at the thought. "And—she told me she killed Sgaire."

Gawen stiffened, closing his eyes before turning to bark an order to a hovering guard.

"Go tae the servants' quarters and see if ye can find Mysie. And send Sgaire's brother tae the castle."

The guard nodded and scrambled away as Gawen returned his focus to her.

"Now she knows Ysenda isn't at her home," Lila continued, her voice filling with panic. "It won't be long before Malmuira heals herself and comes for her. We have to get Ysenda away from here."

"There's a small uninhabited island off of the north coast—my father and uncles used it as a fishing spot. There's a large cottage on the island; we can take Ysenda there."

As Lila nodded her agreement, he gently cupped her face.

"Wait for me in my chamber," he said. "I need tae make arrangements for our departure tae the island at first light."

"Ye need tae tell him ye're with child," Coira urged her in a low voice moments later, as they made their way out of the great hall. Coira was coming with them to the island tomorrow to assist Lila with the spells she needed to perform and was staying in one of the castle's guest chambers.

"I—I will," Lila said, nervousness squeezing her chest.

Once she entered Gawen's chamber, she paced restlessly back and forth. She'd just faced off with the powerful, dark witch she'd been seeking since arriving here, yet she was more anxious about telling Gawen she was pregnant. Would he be upset? Annoyed? Or dare she even hope... happy?

She ended up waiting for what seemed like hours, a multitude of his potential reactions playing over and over again in her mind. She whirled, her heart leaping into her throat when he finally entered. Worry and fatigue haunted his handsome features, and he raked his hand through his already tousled hair.

"I apologize for my delay. There was much tae organize for our departure on the morrow," he said as he approached her. "I should have been with ye tonight," he continued, his eyes shadowing. "I had tae stay here tae reassure panicked nobles. And Struan returned, drunken and angry, determined tae murder his cousin over Ysenda. But that's all handled now, and I'm nae leaving yer side, Lila."

"Malmuira would have killed you if you were with me," Lila said, grief sweeping over her at the thought.

"Had it kept ye safe, I would have given up my life," he vowed.

Tears sprang to her eyes. Again, his words

weren't a vow of love, but she clung to them like a lifeline. Perhaps he wouldn't be upset over the news that she was with child. Perhaps he would ask her to stay with him, to be his wife after she defeated Malmuira.

Her anxiety faded at the hopeful thoughts, and she stepped forward to take his hands.

"Gawen . . . I need to tell you something," she said, holding his gaze, allowing a tentative smile to curve her lips. "I'm with child."

CHAPTER 24

*A*s Lila's words settled in, Gawen stared at her, a torrent of emotions seizing him: shock, joy, fear. Lila was watching him closely, her lovely blue eyes shadowed with anxiety. Of all the swirling emotions that filled him, joy remained, a powerful, all-consuming joy that held him firmly in its grip. He wanted to smile, to pull her into his arms and kiss her, to ask her to be his wife. To be his.

But then the fear settled in. She was a witch from another time, on the verge of going to battle with another powerful witch who'd already tried to kill her. And childbirth was perilously dangerous in this time. He knew of several women who'd died giving birth. His fear rose, chasing away the joy. At least in her own time, she would be safe—and alive. During one of their talks, Lila had told him that modern healers had better medicines to save lives; even childbirth was safer.

"Are ye certain?" he asked.

"Yes," she said, giving him another tentative smile. "Coira helped me confirm."

That joy sprang to life once more, but he tempered it.

"Then ye cannae face Malmuira again. I'll send for another stiuireadh and send ye back. Can ye travel from anywhere or do ye need tae go back tae the grove I found ye in?"

Lila's eyes went wide, and she stumbled back as if he'd slapped her. Her eyes filled with tears, and pain tore at his heart, but he made himself hold firm. Keeping her safe and alive was paramount now that she was with child.

"I'm not going back until I defeat Malmuira," Lila snapped. "That hasn't changed."

"Ye have more than yerself tae think about now," he growled. "'Tis nae safe for the bairn and ye tae—"

"Witches are made to perform magic, I've been performing spells this whole time. None will hurt the baby, especially this early in the pregnancy. And what if this other stiuireadh you send for doesn't arrive in time? I'm not leaving Ysenda, another pregnant woman, to face a murderous witch who wants to kill her."

"She already nearly killed ye!" he roared, panic washing over him. "Ye are nae tae stay here, Lila."

She again flinched as if he'd slapped her, but she raised defiant blue eyes to his.

"I'm not going anywhere yet," she repeated. "I will finish this, and you can't stop me. After I defeat the witch, then—then I'll do as you wish and return to my time. I only wanted you to know."

"I only want ye tae go for yer and the bairn's safety. And ye must ken how dangerous childbirth is in this time."

"Fine. You've made yourself clear, Gawen," she said. Though her voice was hard with anger, there was no mistaking the hurt in her eyes. "You don't want me to stay. I'll go, but only after I defeat Malmuira."

She stormed out of his chamber before he could protest. He wanted to tell her that he did want her, and the bairn, more than anything he'd ever wanted in his life. Yet he couldn't risk losing them both; he would never recover from such a loss.

And now, in the fraught silence Lila had left behind in her wake, he knew why. He loved Lila, his witch from another time. Perhaps he'd loved her since the moment he laid eyes on her in that grove, flushed and wide-eyed and lovely, but he'd tucked it away beneath his overwhelming desire. He loved her, and the best way for him to honor that love, to keep her safe—was to let her go.

∾

"I've never kent ye tae be a fool," Aonghus snapped.

Gawen glared at him. It was the next morning, and after a sleepless night aching for Lila, torn between fear and joy over her pregnancy, he'd awoken and dressed, meeting Aonghus in his study to prepare for the day's journey to the offshore island. He'd told Aonghus about Lila's pregnancy and his determination to send her away; he'd assumed his friend would agree with him.

"Ye're speaking tae yer laird," Gawen bit out. He rarely used his status over Aonghus, but he would have said anything to stop Aonghus from looking at him as if he were the enemy.

"Right now, I'm speaking tae my friend," Aonghus returned, unfazed. "That lass loves ye; anyone with two eyes can see it. Ye've been sleep-walking through yer life since yer family died, and here comes yer first chance at happiness, at a family of yer own, and ye tell her tae leave. So, aye, *Laird* MacRaild. Ye're a fool."

"'Tis nae safe for her during this time," Gawen snapped. "I cannae risk losing her!"

"There is no certainty in anything. I ken how much losing yer family broke ye, but ye cannae let that loss determine the rest of yer life. Do ye think yer family would want ye tae isolate yerself and nae live? They'd want ye tae live, with the lass ye love and yer bairn."

Aonghus gave him one last glare before turning to leave the study, leaving a shaking Gawen in his wake.

Aonghus's words remained in his mind as he and a small group, that included Lila, Coira, Ysenda, Kudan, and the group of men who would act as their guards, departed from the castle, making their way north to where a small fishing boat would take them to the offshore island.

Lila didn't spare a single glance at him during the journey, staying close to Coira, who continually shot him looks of concern.

As their boat departed, he gazed out at the churning sea, imagining Lila living in this time, marrying him and giving birth to his bairn, to a whole host of bairns. A brood of sons and daughters who had her lovely blue eyes.

But this vision of her was paired with that ever-present grief, that blooming fear that kept him captive. What if she didn't survive childbirth? What if Malmuira killed her? What if another plague came to Skye and took her away from him?

He forced the terrifying thoughts away as the boat drew close to the tiny island, rocking violently over the churning waves. Instinct drew him to Lila's side, and he reached out to hold her as she gripped the side of the boat, her face tight with queasiness.

"Are ye unwell?" he asked in a low voice.

"I don't think your son likes sea travel," Lila whispered, clutching her abdomen. His heart lurched, that unfathomable joy seizing him.

"Ye... ye ken 'tis a boy?"

"Just a feeling I have," Lila said shortly, still not looking at him.

Gawen gazed down at her lovely, pale features, torn between that dueling joy and fear, imagining the child who would become his son, and a fierce, possessive pride seized him.

He reluctantly left her side to help his men pull the boat ashore, and they made their way to the lone fishing cottage on the island. It was sizable for a fishing cottage, but there wasn't enough room for everyone to sleep inside. His men and Kudan left the two bedrooms for the women to sleep in while they camped outside the cottage.

While Lila and Coira disappeared into one room and Ysenda into the other, Gawen worked alongside his men, placing them in various spots around the island to patrol the shores for Malmuira's appearance.

He spent the rest of the day patrolling the island with his men, catching glimpses of Lila from a distance as he did so. She and Coira would either work in the kitchen to prepare drafts for Lila's spells, or Lila would perform Protective spells on the outskirts of the cottage. Though Lila was in the early stages of her pregnancy, he could already see the telltale signs, given how well he knew her body—the slight enlargement of her breasts, the iridescent glow of her skin. Pregnancy suited her, making her even more bonnie, and another surge of possessive pride swelled over him; Lila was carrying *his* bairn.

Lila caught him staring at her a few times, a pretty flush staining her cheeks, as if she'd gleaned what he was thinking, before quickly looking away again.

They all ate dinner in the main room of the cottage, a meal of bread paired with ale they'd brought from the castle, along with roasted fish that two of his men had caught earlier in the day. Kudan and one of his guards sat at his side; Lila, Coira and Ysenda sat at the far end of the table, with Lila still not looking at him. Her continual avoidance caused a spiral of pain to tear through him; he could only imagine his anguish when she was back in her own time.

"I want tae apologize," Kudan said in a low voice, pulling him from his painful thoughts. "I'm the reason the dark witch is here on these lands."

Kudan lowered his gaze, shame flickering across his face. There was a time when Gawen would have scolded him for taking another man's wife. But he now knew what it was like to long for a forbidden lass.

"Ye love her, aye?" he asked.

"Aye," Kudan said, tenderness filling his eyes as he gazed at Ysenda. "I was devastated when her father married her off tae my cousin. I tried tae stay away. Ye have tae understand, my laird; it was more than lust. She's become like the air I breathe."

Gawen thought of Lila, her laughter, her dancing, blue eyes. He knew exactly how Kudan felt. He reached out to clamp him on the shoulder.

"There's no need for yer apology," he said. "The only one responsible for what has happened on these lands is Malmuira."

Kudan gave him a grateful smile. Gawen felt Lila's eyes on him and turned, giving her a tentative smile. Her eyes hardened before she turned her attention back to Coira, causing his chest to tighten. But he couldn't blame her for her anger.

After the meal, he made his way out to the cliff's edge, looking out over the churning sea and the darkening sky. He thought again of Aonghus's words, of what his family would have wanted. His fear rose at the thought of losing Lila, but he stymied it, focusing instead on his love for her. Love was the opposite of grief; grief was a coldness, a barren emptiness.

Love was warmth and joy, a joy he'd felt only since she'd come into his life. Lila was the woman who'd appeared out of thin air and landed right in his arms, as if fate itself was telling him that was where she belonged. She was the woman who looked at the world of this time in wonder, who didn't see danger but opportunity. She was the woman who used her magic not for selfish means, but to help others, who, at this very moment, was risking her own life for the sake of another's. She was the woman who would give birth to his bairn.

The woman he loved more than his own life.

The tension ebbed from his shoulders. Once again, Aonghus was right. He had been a fool to allow his fear and grief to rule him. Now was the time to shed the grief that had been his companion for so long, to set his fear from the past aside and live in the present with the woman he loved at his side and their bairn—if she would still have him.

When he entered the cottage, Coira ushered him inside the room she shared with Lila, a knowing smile curving her lips.

"I'm happy tae sleep in the main room by the fireplace. I've plenty of blankets," Coira whispered, leaving the room before he could reply.

Lila was already asleep, curled up in a ball on the narrow bed, her hand resting protectively on her belly. A fierce love and protectiveness washed over him at the sight of her. Lila was his: his family. His home.

He curled up around her in the bed, holding her close, hoping that when she awoke, she accepted his apology, his confession of love—and his proposal of marriage.

CHAPTER 25

*L*ila fell asleep with a heavy heart, aching for Gawen and heartbroken over him wanting to send her away. When she stirred awake just past dawn the next morning, surprise roiled through her; Gawen lay in bed next to her, curled around her body. Her heart lurched as she looked down at his handsome form.

"I love you," she whispered into the silence, not caring that it made her a fool to love a man who was so determined to send her away.

Lila wanted nothing more than to curl back up around him, but she made herself get up, dressing in her loose, dark-green gown and draping a plaid cloak around herself before heading out. She wanted to surround the cottage with even more Protective and Cloaking spells and prepare herself for Malmuira's arrival, which she feared would be sooner rather than later.

She thought that everyone would still be asleep,

but Coira was up and milling about, having made herself at home in the minuscule area by the fireplace that served as a makeshift kitchen.

"Lila, have some bread," Coira urged.

"I should get started with my spells. I won't be long," Lila promised, giving her a polite smile before leaving the cottage.

She knew Coira meant well, but she'd only try to persuade her to talk to Gawen. Coira had been urging her to talk to him since they'd arrived on the island. She figured it was Coira who'd let Gawen into their room last night. But Coira didn't seem to understand that Gawen had explicitly told her he wanted her—and their baby—to leave this time.

Anguish squeezed her chest at the thought, but she ignored the pain as she stepped out into the brisk morning air, determined to fill her mind with spells instead of her heartbreak over Gawen.

After she murmured several Cloaking spells to safeguard the cottage and the still-sleeping Ysenda inside, she tucked her cloak around her body to ward off the early morning chill as she ventured away from the cottage, making her way the small distance along the jagged cliffs until she was out of sight of the cottage. She took in a deep breath, inhaling the damp morning air that smelled of the sea. Coira had prepared her a draft made of terrible-smelling herbs the day before, but it had helped ease her nausea. She almost felt like her pre-pregnant self again.

Lila took in another draw of air, her gaze sweeping over the stunning surroundings. Despite the dire circumstances, it was hard not to admire the island's natural beauty, with its rugged green and brown terrain, the jagged cliffs that plunged into the roaring sea below, the dramatic deep blue sky illuminated by the rising sun.

She moved toward the cliff's edge, taking care to keep a good fifty feet between herself and the very edge which led to a terrifying sheer drop to the sea. There was something oddly familiar about the view, and she took it in for a long moment before lifting up her arms to recite a Defensive spell, one which could help shield her from a magical attack. She closed her eyes as she felt her magic respond to the command of her spell, relishing in the electrical sensation of her power. This was what she was born to do, and despite her setbacks, she allowed herself to take pride in what she had accomplished—identifying Ysenda as the target, wounding Malmuira and buying them more time, arriving safely in this time. She vowed to never let self-doubt cripple her again. Going forward she would relish in the strength she possessed, the power she would pass on to her child. She would teach him—and she had a strong feeling the baby was a boy—to never take his power for granted, to always use his ability as a force for good in this world, a force for love.

Lila's smile froze on her face, her body filling with dread as she sensed a presence behind her. She knew with a dawning horror exactly who it was.

Fear coiled around her spine; how had Malmuira found them so quickly? She thought she'd have more time to prepare.

Lila turned, facing Malmuira. There was no dark triumph in Malmuira's eyes, only a dazed surprise as she stared at Lila's belly. Malmuira shouted a Binding spell before Lila could react, rendering her immobile.

"Ye're with child. I didnae detect it before," Malmuira breathed, as Lila's blood pounded in her ears with panic. "'Tis the only reason I didnae kill ye when yer back was turned."

Disbelief struck Lila. Malmuira was determined to kill Ysenda—another pregnant woman—yet she would spare her?

"Show Ysenda the same mercy," Lila pleaded. She silently issued the spell she'd used to undo the Binding spell before, but this time it didn't take hold, and she remained frozen in place.

The fury returned to Malmuira's eyes as she advanced toward Lila.

"I cannae. Do ye ken I was with child as well? Before the massacre."

Lila blinked, surprise rising beneath her fear and panic.

"What happened?"

She needed to keep Malmuira talking, needed to figure out how to reverse the Binding spell she was under. As soon as she had the chance, she would issue the Killing spell; she'd already attempted to show Malmuira mercy. Never again.

"I was newly married tae my love, Rodric; I'd loved him my whole life, since I was a wee lass. He was excited tae meet his bairn, his son." Malmuira's voice broke as she stepped closer. Lila's panic swelled at her growing proximity; she had to act quickly. "He and other clan nobles attended the feast hosted by a rival clan under the pretense of peace. Our clans had been warring for generations, he wanted it tae end. He wanted peace for me and our bairn—for our family. But the men who invited them tae feast slaughtered him and the others—slitting their throats from ear to ear. I kent exactly when it happened. I awoke with a sharp pain on my neck."

Malmuira's tears were streaming freely now, and beneath Lila's terror, empathy rose. She couldn't imagine losing Gawen in such a brutal way.

"Nae long after his murder, I lost my bairn. My son—our son." Her hand went to her flat belly, fury flashing in her eyes. "I lost everything during that massacre. I have tae stop what is tae come. Ysenda's bairn will give rise tae the events which will come tae pass. She and the bairn must die."

"You know the rules of our kind!" Lila cried. It was no use trying to reason with Malmuira, she was beyond reason. But Lila needed more time to figure out how to counter Malmuira's Binding spell. "There are some events that cannot be changed, no matter how it affects us. The massacre is one of them."

"Would ye nae do everything in yer power tae stop the murder of yer love? The loss of yer bairn?" Malmuira challenged.

Grief constricted Lila's chest at the thought of losing Gawen and her unborn child. She would want to stop it, but she could never resort to what Malmuira had become—she would never resort to murder.

"I wouldn't murder innocent people to stop it!" Lila shouted, her desperation rising. "Malmuira, you don't have to—"

"Enough!" Malmuira snarled. "I ken what ye're doing, but ye willnae stop me. Because ye are with child, I'll give ye a choice. Ye tried tae show me mercy; I'll show ye mercy in kind. Return tae yer time—never return here—and I willnae kill ye."

Lila opened her mouth to protest, but fear coiled around her spine as she saw Gawen, Coira, and his men race toward them. Malmuira sensed their presence, whirling to face them.

"No!" Lila screamed, as Malmuira hurled a spell toward them, sending them all flying dozens of feet backward; they all went still under her Binding spell. But somehow, Gawen evaded her spell, charging forward, his sword withdrawn, expression fierce.

"Gawen!" Lila screamed. "No—"

Malmuira raised her hand, and Gawen halted under the force of her Binding spell. Malmuira studied him with narrowed eyes as rising terror clawed at Lila's heart.

"Please—this is between us," Lila said desperately, trying to get Malmuira's focus back on her.

"This is the father of yer child, I can sense it. Laird MacRaild," Malmuira said, cocking her head to the side. With her petite frame and shrewd gray eyes, she looked like a curious—yet deadly—bird.

"Malmuira, please! Leave him alone. This isn't about him!" Lila screamed.

"If he died in front of ye, ye'll understand my grief. My pain," Malmuira said. Her voice was low, but even over her thundering heartbeat and the roar of the surrounding sea, Lila could hear every word.

"Malmuira—" Lila pleaded, her voice breaking.

"Ye can kill me," Gawen said, his own voice steady, keeping his eyes trained on Malmuira

"Gawen—no!"

Terror ripped through her. She silently issued three spells in succession, but none of them released the Binding spell's hold. Malmuira must have used a Binding spell Lila wasn't familiar with, one she couldn't counter.

"All I ask is for ye tae let Lila go," Gawen continued, ignoring Lila as he kept his focus on Malmuira. "Let her return tae her time, where she'll be safe and can give birth tae my bairn. 'Tis all I want. I—I understand ye, Malmuira. I was like ye once. I lost my entire family tae illness. I begged the stiuireadh to change what happened, and if I had yer power, I would have gone back in time myself tae prevent their deaths. I ken grief. I ken loss."

Malmuira's face crumpled, but she kept her hand outstretched toward him, on the verge of issuing a spell. Helplessness paired with terror had taken hold of Lila, holding her as captive as Malmuira's spell. She couldn't let Gawen die. She couldn't bear it.

"But . . . what I've come tae learn is that loss is a part of life. We all lose; we all love; we all grieve. 'Tis part of life's cycle. What we can do is move on from the loss, from the pain. Tae never forget who we've lost as we open up our hearts again. 'Tis the beauty of life. The magic of love." His green eyes filled with tears and strayed briefly toward Lila. "I was barely living before she came intae my life. I had become so consumed with grief I forgot how tae truly live. But Lila, the lass I love more than my own life, changed that for me. She made me see past the grief. I hope that ye can as well. If ye cannae, all I ask is that ye spare Lila—and Ysenda. If ye need someone tae take out your rage and grief on, take my life."

"Gawen—no!" Lila screamed. "Malmuira, don't listen to him. This is between us, the stiuireadh. Gawen has nothing to do with this!"

Malmuira remained still, her eyes still trained on Gawen. His words must have affected her on some level, because she was shaking, and Lila saw a glimpse of the young woman she must have been before she'd let grief and fury consume her, the young woman who'd been happy and in love, the young woman who'd lost everything in one violent act.

For a fleeting moment Lila hoped that Gawen's words would penetrate, but Malmuira shook her head, her expression hardening once more.

"I've come tae far tae stop now. I willnae just live with my loss—I want back what was taken from me! And I will have it—I will have my husband and my bairn. I was going tae grant yer witch mercy and allow her tae return tae her time, but ye both are standing in my way."

When Malmuira again raised her hand, Lila knew that she would kill Gawen. And it was this terrible certainty that caused a powerful surge to course through her body, as if her magic had picked up on her fear for Gawen, her all-encompassing love. Recalling every single Offensive spell she'd practiced and committed to memory, she threw every ounce of her power into the spells as she shouted several of them at once.

The Binding spell that held her immobile released her from its hold, and as Malmuira opened her mouth to direct the Killing spell at Gawen, Lila darted forward, hurling herself at Malmuira.

Malmuira whirled just as Lila charged forward, raising her hand, and their spells collided, striking them both with such force that they both plunged backward and over the sheer drop of the cliff.

In the terrifying few seconds it took for Lila to realize she was plunging over the edge, she realized why the view had seemed so familiar. She'd seen this cliff and the sheer drop to the sea in the nightmare she'd had before arriving in this time. It was as if this moment—her death—was meant to happen.

At this knowledge, a terrible grief seared her. She would never see Gawen again , never tell him that she loved him, never give birth to the child she already loved so much.

It was the last thought she had before blackness claimed her.

CHAPTER 26

Panic tore through Gawen as he saw Lila plunge over the edge of the cliff. He moved faster than he thought possible, reaching the edge just as Lila plummeted downward, catching her hands and pulling her away from the edge. Below, Malmuira continued to fall until she collided with the rocky shore below, going still as her body let out a sickening crack.

But Gawen's focus was on Lila, his throat constricting with grief. Her eyes were closed, her breathing painfully shallow.

"Lila," he whispered, rocking her in his arms. "Stay with me, my love. I love ye. I love ye so. Both of ye. Please."

He heard Coira and his men approach, now released from Malmuira's spell, but his whole world was the woman in his arms, the woman he would never let go of again.

"Gawen."

Aonghus's hand came to rest on his shoulder. Gawen didn't react, his eyes trained on Lila's sleeping form, his hand gripping her limp one.

It was two days later and Lila still hadn't regained consciousness. Coira had told him the powerful spells she'd performed had taken a toll on her, and she was now in a "coma". In this time, the term was "false sleep." Coira and the healer had ensured him that the bairn was fine, and Lila would be as well, it was just a matter of drawing her out of the coma.

Still, fear gripped him. He'd had an uncle who'd fallen into a false sleep after a hunting accident; he'd never awoken. Gawen hadn't left Lila's side, sleeping in the uncomfortable chair next to her bed, forcing himself to eat meals a servant brought in.

He'd learned from Aonghus that Mysie's body had been found in a nearby forest grove. No one knew where Malmuira had killed and buried Sgaire, his body's whereabouts remained unknown.

As for Malmuira, his men had fetched her body, burying her in an unmarked grave by the old cemetery. Rage burned in his gut at the thought of the dark witch who'd killed innocents on his lands, who'd harmed his Lila. If Lila hadn't killed her, he would have ended her himself.

"Ye havenae eaten today," Aonghus said now, tearing Gawen from his dark thoughts, his voice heavy with concern.

"I've no hunger," Gawen replied, still not taking his eyes off the woman he loved. "Leave me."

Aonghus expelled a sigh; Gawen heard him leave, only to return a few moments later with a tray full of bread, stew, and ale, setting it down on the table next to Lila's bed. Gawen still didn't move, nor tear his eyes away from Lila.

"Ye were right," Gawen murmured, regret constricting his heart. "I was a fool tae push her away. As soon as she told me she was with child, I should have told her how much I loved her. I just—I feared losing her so. But there was no purpose tae avoid telling her how I felt. I may still lose her."

His voice broke, but Aonghus again reached out to grip his shoulder.

"Ye willnae. Yer Lila is strong. She defeated Malmuira; she just needs time tae heal."

Gawen took a shuddering breath, trying to heed his words. Lila's plight was what he'd feared since the moment he realized he had feelings for her, that he would be at her bedside as she fought for her life, just as he'd sat at his family's bedsides. He tightened his grip on her hand, as if that could prevent her from drifting away.

Lila is strong. She will come back tae ye. She must.

Aonghus remained at his side, but to Gawen's relief he didn't talk to him, allowing him to silently hold vigil over his Lila. He recalled her delight at their night picnic, her amusement at his mispronunciation of modern terms, her laughter as she teased him, her eyes trained on his as she lay curled up in bed next to him. He ached to see those blue eyes again, filled with life and laughter and hope. When she awoke, and she would—she had to—he'd take her on an abundance of picnics. An abundance of "dates." He would worship and love her and their bairn for the rest of his days.

Aonghus soon left, and Gawen didn't realize he'd nodded off until he felt a presence in the room behind him.

He turned. A tall, dark-haired woman stood there. He didn't know how, but he sensed she was a stiuireadh. He stumbled to his feet, waiting for the anger and resentment that usually struck him at the sight of a stiuireadh, but none came. He could no longer resent the stiuireadh, not when the love of his life was one of them.

The woman was looking past him at Lila, worry flickering across her face.

"Who are ye?" he demanded. "How did ye get past the guards?"

"I'm Siobhan," she said, unperturbed by his sharp tone, moving to stand by Lila's bedside. "Lila's coven leader."

His tension ebbed. Siobhan, the stiuireadh who'd sent him the letter informing him of Lila's arrival.

"Coira sent me a letter. Even if she hadn't, I detected Malmuira's death. The anomaly is gone, the flow of time restored. Lila achieved what she came here to do."

She gave Lila a look of pride, before concern replaced it. She closed her eyes, and he watched, tense, as she held her hands above Lila.

"What—what are ye doing?"

She ignored him, murmuring a spell beneath her breath. After a few moments, she lowered her hands. Her worried expression had vanished; she looked up at him with a smile.

"She will heal, and your unborn child is well, but you are the one who must draw her out of her coma."

"How?" he rasped. "I'll do anything."

"Talk to her. About anything. Just your voice, and her love for you, will guide her to you," Siobhan said. "I've contacted her family; they'll be arriving here soon. Their presence will help, but it's you who will help her most of all."

"More than her family?"

"Yes," Siobhan said, moving around the bed to approach him. "I'm not one of the matchmaking stiuireadh who send people through time to find their soulmates, but I sensed a thread that linked Lila to this time. I suspected it was you, that she belonged with you. Even if Lila hadn't volunteered to come to this time, I was going to persuade her to. I believe her future has always been in the past—with you."

Warmth spread through him at her words, and she gave him a reassuring smile.

"I know about the loss you suffered. I'm not supposed to tell you this, but I know it's worried you. No other plague will come to Skye in your lifetime. Now that Lila has destroyed Malmuira, Lila will be safe here with you. Now . . . you just have to call her back to where she belongs."

With one last smile she moved past him to the door.

Gawen sat back down at Lila's side, taking her hand, hope skittering through him at Siobhan's words. He turned to thank her, but she'd already vanished. He recalled how Lila had told him that Seers such as Siobhan could rarely travel; they needed to remain in the time they were born to monitor time's flow. It must have been a risk for Siobhan to come to this time, even if it was a brief visit.

He turned his focus back to Lila. While he'd held vigil, he'd not said a word, just listened to the calm, steady hum of her breathing, his fear for her strangling any words that would come. Siobhan's words echoed in his mind. *You just have to call her back to where she belongs.*

He took a breath and began to speak.

He told her everything he could recall about his childhood; petty arguments with Gordana, his intimidation of his father's power and influence, his mother's fierce love for both him and Gordana. He told her of his friendship with Aonghus, how he quickly became the brother he never had, how they would sneak off to the Highlands to shirk their duties, only to be scolded by his father when they returned to Skye. He told her of his sense of growing responsibility as he became a man, knowing that Carraig Castle and Clan MacRaild would one day be his. He told her, only briefly, of his grief over his family's deaths, of his guilt over his survival. But he didn't want to dwell too much on the loss that had once consumed him; he wanted to focus on the light she'd brought into his life.

He delved into everything he'd felt since the moment she arrived in the grove. His instant desire for her, his growing feelings, how he'd foolishly tried to shutter them away. He kept talking, even as Coira and the healer came to check on Lila, even as servants brought him his meals, even as the sky grew dark and his eyes grew heavy with fatigue.

"When ye come back tae me, sweet Lila, I will worship ye for the rest of our days. I will be a good husband tae ye, tae our bairn, tae all the bairns we'll have. I want ye tae marry me, my love. I want ye at my side for always. I love ye. I love ye . . ."

His voice broke, and he closed his eyes, feeling the hot sting of tears. He should never have taken her for granted, never should have tried to push her away. He should have welcomed the love he felt for her for the gift it was.

Gawen stilled when he felt Lila's hand squeeze his. His eyes flew open. Lila's beautiful blue eyes were open and trained on his.

"Lila," he gasped.

She smiled; it was the most glorious sight he'd ever seen. Relief flooded his body: relief and love.

"I heard what you said . . ." Lila's voice was hoarse with misuse. He climbed onto the bed next to her, reaching out to touch her face, hardly believing she was awake again, awake and speaking to him. "I held on to every word. Your words pulled me out of that darkness. I thought . . ." Her voice broke, tears shining in her eyes. "I thought I was dead. I thought I'd never see you again."

"No," Gawen said, his heart constricting at the thought. "I caught you before you fell. I'll always be there tae catch ye—tae pull ye out of any darkness that seeks tae claim ye," he vowed. "I love ye, sweet Lila. I vow tae spend the rest of my days worshipping ye. I want ye tae be my bride, my lady, the mother of all my bairns. I'll never leave yer side. I understand ye need more time tae heal, but I didnae want another moment tae pass without letting ye ken how I feel."

Lila entwined her hands with his, giving him a tremulous smile.

"I don't need more time to know that my answer is yes. It was the thought of your death at her hands that gave me that last burst of strength to defeat her. I love you, Gawen. I want nothing more than to spend the rest of my life with you."

A torrent of joy spread over him, and he leaned forward to press his mouth to hers in a searing kiss; a kiss that promised forever.

CHAPTER 27

Six Weeks Later
Carraig Castle

"I always thought," Avery observed wryly, "that we'd be preparing you for your wedding day in some fancy hotel suite in Raleigh—or New York. I'd never have guessed a fourteenth-century castle chamber. But... I suppose it'll do."

Lila laughed at her sister's quip, trying to hold still as her mother carefully helped her into the sapphire-blue gown that would serve as her wedding dress. Her sister stood opposite her in a period-appropriate, rose gown, clutching a goblet of sweet wine, her blonde hair shining in the midday sunlight that shone in through the chamber window. Though this time period wasn't her favorite, Avery had made herself quite at home.

Lila's family had arrived the same day she'd emerged from her coma, only hours after she'd accepted Gawen's marriage proposal. Avery and her mother had embraced her, grateful tears in their eyes, even as Lila had reassured them she was fine. Her father had been more stoic with his joy, but she'd glimpsed tears in his eyes as he'd held her.

Their reaction to Gawen had been what she'd expected. Avery had dramatically fanned herself and winked after Gawen left the chamber; he'd introduced himself and extended an offer for them to stay in the castle's guest chambers for as long as they wished. Her parents had expressed their admiration at Gawen's kindness and honor, but most importantly, his devotion to Lila. Her family had all been vocal of their approval of her and Gawen's engagement, and expressed genuine joy over Lila's pregnancy.

After awakening from her coma, Lila only took another couple of days to restore her strength, thanks to healing drafts from Coira, along with Healing spells from her mother and Avery. She'd filled her family in on everything that had happened since she'd arrived, worried that her protective parents would insist that she return to the present to have her child, but they'd told her they could see how much Gawen loved her; she was in good hands.

"You didn't have to defeat Malmuira for us to know how strong you are," her father had said, when she'd told them about her hunt for Malmuira and her reasons for doing so. "We've always known that. I'm sorry if I ever made you feel otherwise."

"I know that now," she'd said, giving her father a reassuring smile.

She'd banished that insecurity ever since she'd confronted Malmuira; never would she doubt herself again.

Gawen had played the attentive host to her family during these past few weeks, showing them around the castle and his lands, taking her father out for a hunt, showing Avery and her mother the grove where Lila had arrived, and where the ancient druids had once practiced their rituals.

But he spent most of his time at Lila's side, holding her close in her chamber, or taking walks with her to get air as his hand rested protectively on her belly.

Ysenda and Kudan had paid her a brief visit after her recovery, Ysenda tearfully thanking her for stopping Malmuira. They'd left Skye the previous week, bidding both Gawen and Lila farewell.

Her thoughts returned to the present as Avery set down her wine, her eyes suddenly filling with tears.

"What?" Lila asked, panicked, looking between Avery and her mother. "Is something wrong?"

"No," Avery sniffed. "You just—you look amazing, little sis."

Lila smiled, relaxing. Usually, annoyance would flicker through her for Avery's use of her childhood nickname, but now the endearment filled her with warmth. She met her mother's eyes; they were also filled with tears.

Joy sprang to her heart; she was fortunate that

her family had the ability to travel through time, that they could be with her on her wedding day. Not every stiuireadh or traveler had that luxury.

Lila moved over to the mirror, taking in her reflection with quiet awe. The deep blue of the gown enhanced the color of her eyes; it was high waisted with a low-cut bodice, flattering the curves that the early stages of her pregnancy had already produced. Though it was common for women of this time to wear their hair braided or veiled, she wore her hair loose at Gawen's request. *I want tae wind my hands through it when I make love tae ye on our wedding night*, Gawen had whispered huskily to her the day before. She flushed at the memory of his words, love and desire for her husband-to-be sweeping over her.

"You look so beautiful, sweetheart," her mother whispered, dashing away her tears. "Now. Your handsome Scottish laird awaits. Shall we head down?"

Lila gave her mother a nod, her joy rising at the thought of Gawen waiting for her down in the great hall where their ceremony was to take place.

Lila, Avery, and her mother headed out of the chamber, their arms linked, making their way to the base of the winding stairs, where her father was waiting for her, looking dashing in the belted plaid kilt and tunic he'd taken to wearing in this time.

Her father took her in, the blue eyes she'd inherited glistening as he linked his arms with hers.

"Are you ready, sweetheart?" he asked.

"More than ready," she whispered.

He beamed at her, and together they entered the great hall where their guests awaited. Lila's entire focus was on Gawen, who stood at the head of the hall next to the priest. Her breath hitched, her love for him coursing through her veins. He seemed to grow more handsome by the day; he wore his finest white tunic and a belted plaid kilt of deep blue to match her gown. He straightened, his green eyes filling with admiration and love as she approached.

The ceremony went by in a blur; they recited their vows in both English and old Gaelic. When the priest announced they were wed, tears of happiness pricked her eyes as she gazed up at her new husband. Her love.

Gawen grinned, reaching out to swing her up into his arms, pressing his lips to hers in a searing kiss.

"Now . . . I have tae fulfill my promise of worshipping ye every day," he murmured, when they broke apart.

Lila laughed and nodded her agreement as he kissed her once more. An all-encompassing joy swept over her, a joy she relished in, knowing she was right where she belonged.

CHAPTER 28

*A*very watched her sister dance with her new husband, happiness spiraling through her at the pure joy in Lila's eyes. Lila had always given herself a hard time over her magic; she was glad to see her sister finally accept and appreciate her power—and find love with a hunky Scottish laird who clearly adored her.

"Will we be attending your wedding next?" Avery's mother teased.

Avery laughed, shaking her head. She enjoyed her freedom too much to even remain in one time period for too long; she doubted she would ever get married.

"I think Lila has taken on the mantle of supplying you and Dad with grandchildren," Avery said, with a playful wink.

Her father chuckled, taking her mother's hand as they stood to dance.

"We'll see about that, young lady."

He winked at her as he guided her mother to the center of the great hall where other couples were dancing. As she watched both couples, Lila and Gawen, and her parents, the envy that surged through her took her by surprise.

She shook her head, ignoring it. Avery took pride in her freedom, in the ability to hop to various time periods. She couldn't imagine committing to just one, something that marriage usually required.

Raising her glass of wine to her lips, Avery froze when she glimpsed a tall, broad-shouldered man at the far end of the hall. She was too far away to see him clearly, but she was certain that his gaze was trained on her.

Without thinking, Avery set down her wine and lurched to her feet, moving through the sea of dancing bodies to step out of the great hall, looking up and down the empty corridor. There was no sign of the mystery man, no sign of anyone. But as she turned to head back inside, she couldn't escape the feeling—the utter certainty—that the man was out there somewhere . . . waiting for her.

∽

LATER, as the wedding festivities died down and Gawen carried a blushing Lila out of the great hall, Avery bid good night to her parents, who made their way up to their guest chamber. She was still flush with wine and unsettled by her glimpse of the mystery man; she needed to take in some air.

Avery made her way out to the courtyard, still

bustling with activity as wedding guests made their way to the stables or out the front gate. She took in the starry night sky above, moving to the edge of the courtyard to get away from the drunken conversations of the guests.

She stilled as she looked out the front gates of the courtyard. A young woman stood there, on the far edge of the castle grounds, staring directly at her.

Avery froze, unease creeping down her spine. What was it about this time? First the mystery man, now this mystery woman.

Determined not to let her slip from view, Avery made her way out of the front gate, approaching the edge of the grounds where the woman stood. She was young, possible a decade younger than Avery's twenty-eight years, with ash-blonde hair and amber eyes that verged on gold. Avery halted, knowing instinctively that this was a fellow stiuireadh.

"Ye're Avery," the young woman said, training those unsettling golden eyes on her.

"Yes," Avery replied, her heart picking up its pace. "How do you know my name? Did someone send you?"

"I take it ye've seen him?" the young woman continued, as if she hadn't spoken at all.

Avery stiffened; she had to be referring to the mystery man.

"Who—who is he?" Avery asked haltingly.

"Laird of Arran Isle," the young woman replied, with a kind, benevolent smile. She reached out to take her hands and Avery shivered; they were ice cold. "He needs yer help. I'm taking ye tae him."

And before Avery could react, or even glean what was happening, the young woman murmured a spell, and the world around her disappeared—plunging Avery into the unknown.

~

READ BHALTAIR'S *Pledge (Highlander Fate, Lairds of the Isles Book Two) now.*

GLOSSARY

Below please find a glossary of magical terms used in the novel.

aingidh - a stiuireadh who uses magic for dark purposes

aosu tapa - the aging and de-aging process that affects some stiuireadh, giving them the appearance of seeming much older—or younger—than their actual age, all in the space of minutes

Arsa grimoire - an ancient grimoire containing powerful spells used by stiuireadh

fiosaiche - Seers who can detect anomalies in the flow of time

glamour - an enchantment used to take on the appearance of another person

GLOSSARY

Pact - the agreement between the stiuireadh and the chieftains of the Scottish isles pledging to assist the stiuireadh in times of need

Seer - see *fiosaiche* above

sidhe - a term for fairies in Scottish and Irish mythology

stiuireadh - a witch or witches who possess the ability to travel through time

Tairseach - a time-travel portal located in the Scottish Highlands

ALSO BY STELLA KNIGHT

Highlander Fate Series

Eadan's Vow

Ronan's Captive

Ciaran's Bond

Niall's Bride

Artair's Temptress

Latharn's Destiny

Highlander Fate Omnibus Books 1-3

Highlander Fate, Lairds of the Isles Series

Gawen's Claim

Bhaltair's Pledge

Domhnall's Honor

ABOUT THE AUTHOR

Stella Knight writes time travel romance and historical romance novels. She enjoys transporting readers to different times and places with vivid, nuanced heroes and heroines.

She resides in sunny southern California with her own swoon-worthy hero and her collection of too many books and board games. She's been writing for as long as she can remember, and when not writing, she can be found traveling to new locales, diving into a new book, or watching her favorite film or documentary. She loves romance, history, mystery, and adventure, all of which you'll find in her books.

Stay in touch! Visit Stella Knight's website to join her newsletter.

Stay in touch!
stellaknightbooks.com

Made in United States
Orlando, FL
29 August 2024